THE BOSS + THE MAID = CHEMISTRY

LOUISE BAY

Published by Louise Bay 2024

ISBN – 978-1-80456-033-4

Private Player

Dr. Off Limits

Standalones

Hollywood Scandal

Love Unexpected

Hopeful

The Empire State Series

Gentleman Series

The Wrong Gentleman

The Ruthless Gentleman

The Royals Series

The Earl of London

The British Knight

Duke of Manhattan

Park Avenue Prince

King of Wall Street

The Nights Series

Indigo Nights

Promised Nights

Parisian Nights

Faithful

Sign up to the Louise Bay mailing list at

www.louisebay/mailinglist

Read more at www.louisebay.com

ONE

Bennett

Some people might call me paranoid. I prefer terms like *careful. Private. Discreet.*

"Anyone ever tell you, you're fucking paranoid?" Leo asks as he crashes into the main living area of my hotel suite. Apparently *some people* includes one of my closest friends.

"Help yourself to a drink." I nod toward the bar and snap my laptop closed. It's nearly eight. Leo's always early. Byron's always late, though he's not coming at all tonight. The rest of them are pretty on time.

"Did you fire the whole staff?" he asks. "Are you so paranoid that it's only you living at this hotel now?" He pulls out a beer from the fridge.

"You're too good to get your own beer?" I ask.

He shrugs and prizes off the bottle top. "You want to tell me why you moved into your own hotel? Why we can't go out to a bar?"

"Things are... difficult for me at the moment."

Leo might think a drink in a bar or even a private

members club would be more enjoyable, but I can't take the risk. I've got way too much to lose.

"Have you thought about wearing a mask out in public?" he asks.

I narrow my eyes, trying to assess whether he's serious. "Like... Batman?"

He pauses, tosses the bottle opener onto the counter and heads toward me. "I think the little ears on top might be a step too far. Plus, people might expect you to fight crime and shit. But you could wear a Covid mask. Pretend you're at risk or something."

The door opens again and Jack and Fisher appear, closely followed by Worth. I look at my watch. It's exactly eight.

Fisher heads over and we exchange a hug. Fisher is a big smiler and a big hugger. It probably means we all hug more than we would have without him in the group. But despite his affability on the surface, he's razor sharp and takes no prisoners. The phrase "wolf in sheep's clothing" was invented for him. Maybe it's because he's British, but I'm always surprised when I hear of his ruthlessness. As much as I love him, I wouldn't want to sit across from him at a boardroom table.

"You okay, bud?" he asks, looking me in the eye.

The last few days have been tricky. Fisher's the first one I called.

"Did we agree that it's okay to actually live in the hotel?" Jack asks. "Doesn't that give you an unfair advantage or something?"

I push my hands through my hair. Sometimes I feel like the dad of the group. Other times I feel like the dartboard, and they're all taking aim. It's gonna be a long night. "I don't need an advantage. This hotel has outperformed all *your* hotels for the last three years. Three years when I didn't live here."

Each of us own a hotel, bought with a very small portion of the proceeds from the sale of a jointly held company we set up in business school. It was a way of keeping us connected while encouraging the healthy competition we all crave. It's an ongoing, friendly-slash-brutal contest that also makes us a little money.

Fisher eyes the whisky bottle and ice bucket on the table in front of me, then grabs a lowball from the bar. That's the thing with Fisher—you can't ever tell in advance what he's going to drink. I swear it's a metaphor for his personality.

"Maybe *I'll* live in *my* hotel," Leo says. His British accent always seems to get more pronounced when he's agitated.

There are two Brits and four Americans among us. As far as I'm concerned, the British are over-represented. Didn't we throw them out already?

"You'd get evicted," Fisher says. "Too many guest complaints about weird sex noises."

Leo grins. "What can I say? I make women scream in the bedroom." He doesn't mind his reputation as a total man-whore. Leo is the opposite of me in so many ways: a regular feature in the gossip columns, careless, indiscreet. There's no stiff upper lip as far as Leo is concerned.

"Yup, when they see the tiny dick they're going to have to deal with," Worth says as he hits the couch with his beer. Worth is a man of few words, but every single one of them is on point.

I aim the TV controller at the wall in front of me and flip to ESPN. We won't actually watch much of whatever's on. Monday night catch-ups started because Jack suggested watching Monday Night Football together. But our weekly get-togethers have never been about sports. It's just an excuse to get together with five people we trust. No one tells you that the richer you get, the lonelier you get. I've always known it, because I saw it with my mom—surrounded by people, but they all wanted something from her: a slice of her fame, a cut of her wealth, one or two of her connections. It even extended to me—kids at school wanting to be my friend in the hopes they'd catch a glimpse of, or exchange a few words with, a movie star.

It's not that I wasn't proud of my mom—I was. She was a phenomenal actress and savvier than many, careful with the projects she chose and the money she made from them. I just didn't understand the allure of fame. I didn't get why she enjoyed everyone looking at her, people hanging on her every word. Maybe I saw that it wasn't *her* they were inter-ested in, just the gilded version of her she let them see. A version they created in their minds. It didn't concern her why they were interested; she drank down the attention like she was constantly parched.

True, deep, authentic friendships are hard to find, and the six of us know it. There's an unspoken understanding among us that regular gatherings nourish our bond. None of us wants to lose it. We know what we've got is rare.

"How long are you going to stay here?" Fisher asks.

"I don't know," I reply. "I need to understand if the break-ins at my apartment building are aimed at me."

"They didn't try to get into your apartment, though, did they?" Leo asks. He takes everything at face value. Some-times I wonder how he's made so much money. Because money is always made in the space between ideas.

"No. Just the two apartments under mine," I reply.

"So that's good, isn't it?" Leo asks.

"Depends on what the goal is," Worth says.

Exactly.

"Why don't you just move? Like, get a new apartment?" Leo asks.

I sigh and my chest sinks as I relax. Now they're here, I feel like I can take off the metaphorical masks I wear and finally be myself.

"I might have to move in the end," I say. "But I want to get rid of the problem first. I want to figure out whether the break-ins are linked to me, who's tracking me if they are, and what they want."

"I can answer that for you," Fisher says. "Every tech firm in America is tracking you and they want what you have and they don't—the Midas touch."

I groan at the mention of the Greek king. I first got the moniker from the tech press when my company, Fort Inc., sold the technology for mapping the entire world to a well-known tech firm in Mountainview, California. It caught on in the mainstream press when Fort became the fifth-largest privately owned company in America. I hated it because I've tried hard not to make Fort about me. It's the last thing I want—partly because it underplays the role my hugely talented staff have, and also because I have no interest in the fame and publicity that comes alongside that kind of nickname.

"Make it make sense," Leo says. "You live in New York City and you think your building getting broken into twice is about you? Maybe we can skip past the paranoia box and tick narcissism."

I sigh, resigned to the fact that I'm going to have to explain it to convince Leo. I'm pretty sure Leo's approach to business is to yap at people like a chihuahua with a caffeine addiction until the people he's dealing with surrender and give him what he wants.

"Before these last two break-ins, my building had been broken into once in the last five years. Its security is second to none downtown. The one break-in years ago was opportunistic—residents left the goddamn window open and they lived on the first floor. Fast-forward to two weeks ago, when the two apartments underneath mine get broken into. There's no connection between the owners of the two apartments, and nothing of value was stolen. But if someone wanted to track my movements, plant listening devices, cameras or god knows what else, an apartment abutting mine would be the place to start."

"And they're after Ben Fort?" Worth asks. Ben Fort—the pseudonym I invented after my mother died—is the CEO of Fort Inc.

I shrug. "No one's interested in Bennett Fordham."

"Unless maybe someone's made the connection between the two?" Worth asks.

I take a sip of whisky as I revisit the question that I ask myself on a daily basis. "I don't think so. If they had, I think I would have read about it. But they may have made a connection between my *apartment* and Ben Fort. That's the first step. They may or may not have a photograph of me."

"But you always wear a hat coming or going," Fisher says.

"Yeah, but that's so any street cameras don't get a shot. Someone with a telephoto lens could get a picture easily."

"You think they've tracked everyone coming in and out of your office building and followed them home and thought to themselves, that's Ben Fort?" Fisher asks. "I mean it might be possible if you worked at some downtown building with a hundred people in it. But your offices are at the Time

Warner building or the Deutsche Bank Center or whatever the fuck they're calling it now. There are thousands of people coming and going from that place every day."

"All right," I say. "Maybe they haven't tracked me that way. Maybe they've made the connection some other way. But my gut tells me whoever broke into the building this week knows Ben Fort lives there. Because Ben Fort justifies two break-ins in a matter of weeks. Most people don't. If they don't get in, they go somewhere else. It kind of doesn't matter if they know I'm him at this point."

Worth pulls in a deep breath. That normally means he disagrees with whatever is being said.

I get it. I sound paranoid. There's no hard evidence for anything, just my gut feelings.

All of us have varying degrees of fame associated with our kind of wealth. Leo is the most high profile, but Fisher definitely courts publicity. He has to. It's part of the deal when you're in the music business. I really do get it, and I don't judge any of them for wanting the advantages a high profile can bring. It's just I don't.

I have no interest in being a household name like Elon Musk or Mark Zuckerberg. I can't think of anything worse. My mother would have loved it. And if anyone finds out who Ben Fort, "Midas touch" owner of Fort Inc., is and especially if he's Bennett Fordham, son of movie star Kathleen Fordham, that's exactly what will happen. I'll go back to the days of paparazzi jumping out of bushes to get a photo, back to people wanting to get close to me, hoping the fame and money will rub off on them.

I'm not prepared to let that happen. The only good thing about my mother dying when I was nineteen was that the press and paparazzi lost interest in me.

I don't want them back.

"Do you have a plan other than hiding out until people lose interest?" Jack asks. "Because if that's your plan, I have to tell you, it's not great."

"I have people watching my apartment." That grossly understates the team of people I have scouring the area—physically and electronically—to find evidence that my building is being surveilled. My security team is the best of the best. Realistically, I'm not going to go back to that apartment, but at the same time, there doesn't seem much point in moving if I'm going to be discovered again.

"Worst-case scenario, people make the connection," Jack says. "Okay, so they'll be interested for a minute. I hate to tell you, Bennett, but they're going to get bored real quick when they find out you're just not that interesting."

I tap my bottle against Jack's. "Cheers to that."

"Son of a Hollywood legend, youngest ever self-made billionaire according to *Forbes*," Jack goes on. "Loyal, too good-looking, wouldn't want to arm wrestle him, and the best friend a man could ever want. Apart from that, you're as dull as the bottom of my shoe. Really. Take comfort from the fact that if you do get found out, they'll quickly lose interest."

"You're an asshole," Worth says, on point again.

"Maybe," Jack replies. "But I'm not telling any lies."

If I didn't know Jack, I'd think he was *just* being an asshole, but that's not his only intention. He's genuinely trying to make me feel better. The five of them have known about my mother since business school. Only Jack has ever told me I shouldn't hide.

"Look," Leo says. "I don't mind the attention."

Worth sniggers and I raise my eyebrows. Leo *loves* the attention.

"Fisher, too, to a lesser extent," he says, completely

ignoring our amusement. "But that's part of our show. Doesn't mean you have to do the same. You gotta live your life."

He doesn't get it. This *is* me living my life. It's just a life that doesn't involve socializing in public places at the moment.

But it's not forever.

"At least have the occasional drink at the hotel bar."

"No!" Leo says. "That will give him more advantage."

I'm the only one of the six of us who keeps his identity from the hotel manager and staff. The Avenue's manager knows the owner is Ben Fort, but because no one's ever seen him, no one realizes he's currently booked into the Park Suite. I've checked in under my real name, Bennett Fordham. I didn't take the Presidential Suite—that would attract too much attention.

Staying here probably does give me a competitive advantage in our little game. I imagine the staff at other hotels give slightly different service when they know they're dealing with the owner. I'm interested in how the hotel operates, warts and all.

"Yeah, maybe we should meet in the bar next week," I say and enjoy the way Leo shoots Jack a look that could kill. Our competition is only friendly-ish. We all want to win and no one wants to give anyone else an advantage, even if it's a night racking up a large bill in the hotel bar.

"I wouldn't take the risk," Leo says. "You've managed to keep your identity secret up until now. Why chance it?" He's smiling as he speaks. We all know he's trying to steer us away from spending money in The Avenue. But honestly, they're drinking from my hotel bar as we speak. It doesn't make a lot of difference.

"The six of us together would attract a lot of attention," Worth says. He's right. As ever.

"As long as that attention is female with legs for days, I'm okay with it," Leo says.

"Don't worry," Worth says. "You can have third pick after Bennett and me."

"I'll give you Bennett," Leo says. "He's too fucking handsome and he's got that brooding hero thing down. But you think women are going to pick you before me?" He scoffs.

I groan and turn up the volume on the TV. We're already in competition in business. We don't need to be competing over women. I need to save my energy.

Leo punches my arm in a friendly way as he gets up to get another drink. "If there's anything I can do, let me know."

Over the last decade, Fort Inc. has successfully developed some of the most important technology in the world. And I've managed to lead that company without anyone knowing I'm the son of a movie star. I need to figure out who's behind the break-ins and silence them. Then we can go back to Monday nights at an exclusive private members club, and my friends can stop bitching about how great my hotel is.

TWO

Efa

New York, New York. A city so great they named it twice—
though it seems a little unnecessary to me. I mean, *we get it.*
It's New York. No need to repeat yourself.

Anyway, here I am in New York City. It's almost like
I'm standing in a cartoon. Or on a film set. I've seen it on
TV and in films so many times that I convinced myself the
version of the city I knew couldn't be real. But the cabs
really are that yellow and steam really does balloon up from
manhole covers. Everything's bigger than it is back in
London. Louder. The skyscrapers are so tall they block out
the sun, and everyone shouts, including the guy who served
up my coffee this morning. He either had anger management problems or was particularly frustrated to be working
the weekend.

I lean back on the stone wall behind me and gaze up at
the building in front of me, on the other side of Columbus
Circle. It houses the headquarters—and only office—of Fort
Inc., the most successful technology company in corporate

history. It's not listed on the stock exchange, and the owner —Ben Fort—doesn't court publicity. In fact, he shuns it. There are no pictures of him on the internet. I can't even fathom being powerful enough to be able to scrub the internet clean of me. He doesn't have a LinkedIn page, and bizarrely for a tech company, Fort Inc. doesn't have a website. No one knows how you get a job there or who they employ.

But I like a challenge.

Fort Inc. fascinates me. Over the last few years, they've produced some of the most revolutionary products the industry has ever seen. AI basically wouldn't exist if it wasn't for Fort. Which is why I want to work for them. With my shiny new degree in computer science, I'm still figuring out what I want to do in the technology space. I know I want to make an impact, I'm just not quite sure how yet. To figure it out, I want to work with the best of the best.

And that's Fort Inc.

I spend the next twenty minutes trying to cross Columbus Circle and finally reach the entrance to the Deutsche Bank Center. I don't have a plan. Today is all about seeing a little of New York before I start work tomorrow morning, but I couldn't *not* come here. I could just turn up at Fort Inc. reception and say I want a job. What have I got to lose? Problem is, I don't know what floor they're on. Maybe they don't even *have* a reception.

I make my way through the throng of tourists and get to the office lobby. Maybe I'll get lucky and find Fort Inc. listed on a building directory. I'll casually breeze past and bump into the head of HR.

Rumors say Fort hand-selects people from the best colleges and others making their mark in the industry. I went to university on the other side of the ocean and I only just turned twenty-one, so there's not much chance of me getting noticed by them, or anyone. But in my experience, tenacity pays off. By the end of the summer, I'm determined to be working for Fort Inc.

In the meantime, I get to enjoy a summer in New York —although I hear it can be humid—while working in one of the best hotels in the city, The Avenue.

I get into the lobby and scan the walls for a directory, but it's all backlit marble and looks more like a spa than a reception space.

"Can I help you?" asks a small woman from behind one of the two mammoth desks that run either side of the lobby.

I stride toward her. "Actually, I was wondering what floor Fort Inc. is on?"

Her expression is blank and she turns to her computer screen. "I'm sorry, we have no record of that company here."

I pause before I respond. I can't tell if she knows she's bullshitting me or not. Like, has she never heard of Fort Inc.? Do they rent this place incognito? Or is she used to being asked and making an excuse to get rid of people? Either way, there's no point in pushing it. I smile. "Thanks." I turn and head out the door.

I didn't expect it to be easy, did I?

It's getting late and the only other thing I had planned was to check out the hotel where I'll be working for the next few months. Lucky for me, one of my sister's inherited brothers-in-law has an apartment in New York City, where I'll be staying. It also happens to be a block from the hotel, situated on Fifth Avenue overlooking the park. Lucky me.

I cut through Central Park to reach the hotel. It probably takes twenty minutes, but all the new sights and sounds eat away at the time. In what feels like seconds, the doorman of The Avenue is welcoming me inside the elegant lobby.

My joining instructions say the staff entrance is East 60th Street, and I make a mental note to head back to my borrowed apartment that way, just so I can check it out.

The lobby is huge, much bigger than I'd expected looking from the outside. It's all dark wood and red thick-pile carpet. A dramatic arrangement of exotic purple flowers fills a circular mahogany table, and three reception-ists in black suits stand behind the dark, built-in desks to the right.

I don't want to ask any of the staff where the bar is just in case they recognize me tomorrow. It might look like I'm spying on them. Instead, I follow two middle-aged women with very expensive handbags. Luckily, we're all headed for cocktails.

The bar continues the dark theme, accented with gold and bronze. There are plenty of clandestine corners for elicit affairs and a semicircular bar that looks like it's floating in the middle of the room. It's moody and sexy and I'm here for it. I'll probably be here cleaning it tomorrow, but for now, I'm a customer.

I slide onto one of the barstools and a barman immedi-ately hands me a cocktail menu. Before I can wonder how the hell I'm going to read it in such a dimly lit space, he produces a torch and shines it so I can choose what I want to drink. Is it me, or is it a little awkward having him just stand there while I decide? "Can I hold the torch?" I ask.

There's a subtle rumbling sound that makes the bar vibrate, and I wonder if we're situated over a tube... er, metro... no, *subway station*. If I didn't know we were in New York and not California, I'd think we were experi-encing a small earthquake.

A tall man in a navy suit slides onto the barstool next to me on the right and the rumbling stops.

Was it him? Was *he* making the sound?

"Of course," the barman says, handing me the torch and distracting me from my thoughts.

The cocktails look, well, delicious. I'd quite happily take any of them. "What do you recommend?" I ask the barman, just as he sets down a drink in front of the man who seemed to make the bar quake.

How did he get served so quickly? He must be a regular. I've never done any bartending before. I hope Gretal doesn't expect me to come with any kind of useful skill set. Gretal is the hotel manager and friend of my soon-to-be brother-in-law's brother. Does that make him *my* brother-in-law? Like, do I inherit six brothers-in-law or do I only get the brother who's marrying my sister? I make a mental note to Google it when I get back to my apartment. Tapping my phone in this bar right now would light the place up like a Christmas tree and I'm trying to go unnoticed.

"Do you prefer vodka-based cocktails or gin?" he asks.

"I like vodka. I like gin." Sounds like the beginning of a subversive children's nursery rhyme that I'll teach my niece, Guinevere, as soon as she can talk.

"I suggest Vagabond Shoes," he says.

I scan the ingredients and don't find anything I don't like. Although, unless they were serving a cocktail with broccoli in it, it's unlikely I'd find anything that would put me off. "Sounds good."

The barman waits a beat for me to hand him back the torch before he sets about pulling bottles from backlit shelves and pouring their contents into a cocktail shaker.

Out of the corner of my eye, the man to my right leans back in his chair. I turn slightly and meet his gaze. My heart turns inside out in my chest as his gaze burns into me and the vibrations that I felt earlier start again. This time, I'm very clear on the fact it's not a subway train or an earthquake. It's definitely him making that sound. It's like he's... growling.

At me.

And I can feel it tugging between my legs.

Even though he's sitting down, I can tell he's tall. And big. Not beefy big. He doesn't look like an American footballer. He's just... gorgeous. And American-looking, if that's a thing. It's weird because even if I wasn't sitting in a five-star hotel, and he wasn't wearing a custom suit and an expensive watch, I would know he was rich from his haircut. His almost-black hair is on the long side of short, swept up and back like someone blow-dried it for him. And if they didn't? Jesus, I'd take that kind of volume on a daily basis.

"What's your name?" he asks, and I realize I'm staring.

"Eddie," I reply.

He shakes his head. "What's your full name?"

"Everyone calls me Eddie."

He glances away and shifts in his seat so he's leaning on the bar, like he's done with our conversation.

"What's *your* name?" I ask him. He may be finished with me, but I'm far from finished with him.

He shakes his head again. "I asked first."

I laugh but he doesn't respond. He's serious.

The barman slides my drink in front of me and I take a sip. The taste doesn't even register. All I can think about is the guy next to me.

I don't ever tell anyone my real name. I've even thought about changing it. I've never liked it. I could make something up, but why should I? If I tell this guy my name's Eddie, my name's Eddie.

I take another sip of my drink, and I can't help but stare at his profile. His jawline is covered with a couple of days' growth and it looks good on him, but there's something in the lines at the side of his eyes and the edge of his lips that tells me he's had a bad day. Maybe a bad year.

"You don't like the name Eddie?" I ask.

He turns so our gazes lock again and then moves closer, so he's talking directly in my ear. "You like what you see. I like what I see. But I'm not going to fuck you until I know your real name."

A low throb beats between my thighs and I exhale shakily. Did he really just say that to me? I mean, I know New Yorkers have a reputation for being direct, but a comment like that sounds extreme and... completely sexy.

And how does he know I'm interested? Hmm. It's probably not that difficult to surmise, given my staring.

He turns back to the bar, leaving me with a choice. I can enjoy the rest of my cocktail and ignore the guy next to me, or I can tell him my name—or a made-up name that I prefer —and get laid.

"Efa," I say, without thinking. I've not said it out loud for a long time. Do I dislike it because my parents chose it, and my generalized resentment for them has bled through to my name? Or maybe because it sounds so feminine, so weak? Either way, it's my real name.

That growl again.

"I'm Bennett," he says.

"Good to know," I say.

Nothing like a bit of American confidence. I had an American boyfriend for about three and a half weeks when I was seventeen. It's like the confidence is hard-wired—part of their genetics. It was irritating on Brad. On Bennett though? It makes me wonder how his hand will feel sliding over my stomach. How his tongue will feel on my neck. Whether the vibrations from his growl could actually make me come.

"I'm a lesbian," I say and turn back to my drink.

"No you're not. You're interested in me. I'm interested in you. Let's not waste time pretending otherwise."

I turn back to him with narrowed eyes. "Okay," I say. "I'm *potentially* interested in you. You seem..." I lean back a little so I can take him all in. "Interesting." I pause and appreciate the fact that he doesn't respond with, "In all the right places." I guess I'm used to boys in their twenties and this *man* here is definitely not in his twenties. "Haven't made up my mind about whether I want to have sex with you yet."

He gives a smirk bordering on arrogant or condescending or something, but just misses. "Okay, well, when you figure it out, let me know." He takes a sip of his drink and I do the same, mirroring him. I don't know if this cocktail is the strongest thing I've ever tasted, but I swear, the body on this guy is making me weak. Everything about him is attractive. The broad shoulders that make me feel tiny. The large hands that hold his glass like it's a child's tea set. The sharp jawline that might be too much if it wasn't for those full, soft lips. No doubt he has a fantastic arse from all that time he so obviously spends in the gym.

"You have to woo me," I announce.

"I'm not trying to date you," he replies. "This is just about sex."

My nipples pinch as he says the word *sex*, like it's forbidden.

"Right." I tap my temple. "Sex is ninety percent a mind game."

"Not the kind of sex I like." His eyebrow quirks, and I

squeeze my thighs together as I imagine him closer, so close I can feel his breath on my neck.

Maybe him saying something like that should be off-putting, like sex is a sport to him, but I can't help being intrigued. What's the kind of sex he likes? And would I like it?

But I'm not afraid to make him work for it. Just a little. "So you just want a hole?" I ask and wince, hoping it's not the case.

"That's not what I said," he says, his voice lowered as he stares at me. How can just a look from a man be the reason my skin is covered in goose bumps? "Sex is physical." He draws the words out and it's intense, like he's reading the work of ancient philosophers.

I need to lighten the mood. "Are you into whips and chains and stuff?" I ask.

He pauses. "Are you?"

I pull in a breath as I consider his question. "Not so far. But I wouldn't rule it out. If I really liked a guy, I'd probably give it a go. But I think I'd know by now if that was my thing, wouldn't I?" I look at him expectantly. He's older. He should know about these things.

He chuckles. "I have no idea. But as humans, I think we should allow ourselves room to grow and change."

"Right," I say, studying him. I wasn't expecting him to answer me properly. Definitely not with an answer so profound. It feels like he really believes that. That we're all capable of growing. "I like that idea," I say. "Everyone expects children to grow and change and then suddenly you're grown up and you're just meant to stop. It's human nature to evolve, right? I have so many things I want to do— lots of different things. Why do I have to limit myself?"

"You *don't* have to limit yourself," he replies. "Not with me, anyway."

Something settles in me. I smile up at him. It's a smile that says, hey, I like you, you're interesting.

"Be careful with that thing," he says and takes another sip of his drink.

"What thing?" I ask.

"Your smile. Use it wisely."

My eyes flick to the line of spirits at the back of the bar so he can't see quite how much I enjoyed his compliment.

"Wisely? Is it a weapon? You think it's my superpower?"

He glances all the way down to my feet and back up, his gaze a blowtorch and I'm ice. I soften and melt, feeling my fight disappear.

"I think you have many powers," he says, his tone gravelly, his eyes heated.

"Maybe I'll go through a spanking phase or whips or whatever," I say, slower now. My mind is so full of him, I'm struggling to form a thought. "I'm just not there now." I pause, wondering if that's what he expects. "Is that a deal-breaker for you?"

"Not a dealbreaker," he replies. "It's not my kink either."

Thank god.

"Anything else I should know?" I ask.

He gives me that smirk again. "I'm beginning to suspect I shouldn't even try to guess what you think you should know."

"Good assumption." I consider whether there's other incidental information we should share before I take him up on his offer. Because I really want to see this guy naked. I really want those large hands roaming my body. I really want to know what a more experienced man, a man who looks and talks like he does, could do to me. "Do you have condoms?" I ask. "And where do you live? I'm a block away."

He doesn't reply. He turns back to the bar and gestures for the barman. He signs off two bills and stands. "Let's go," he says. "I'm downtown. Let's go to your place."

THREE

Bennett

The first thing I noticed about her was her waist, and how her ass flared out as she sat. But the moment I decided I wanted to fuck her was when she brought her tongue to her lips, deep in thought. It gave me an instant hard-on.

Then she started talking. And somehow that didn't put me off like it usually does.

"Nice place," I say as I glance around at her apartment. I didn't tell her I was staying at the hotel. I just said my place was downtown. Not a lie.

"Thanks. It's not mine. I'm borrowing it while I'm in New York." I know she's telling the truth. For some reason, I can feel in my bones that this woman can't lie. She doesn't have it in her.

With the British accent, it makes sense that she doesn't live in New York. All the better for me. I don't like the possibility of running into women I've slept with. Not unless it's intentional.

"I'm having a summer of fun," she says. "Doing lots of

different jobs. You know? Like you said, I don't believe in limiting myself."

She could be me at twenty. As a kid, family and friends would ask me what I wanted to do when I "grew up". Ironic, given my mother played pretend for a living until she died at forty-four. I used to give a different answer every time—doctor, explorer, superhero. Not because I had changed my mind, but because I wanted to do all those things. That's what's so great about tech. It encompasses so much, from medicine to maps and everything in between.

She faces me wearing a full-on smile, like she's a movie heroine returning home to find her lover waiting at the airport with a big sign. Except she's not acting. There's nothing affected about her smile. Her genuineness nudges something awake inside me that's been long dormant.

I slide my hand across my chest, trying to push the feeling away.

"You okay?" she asks, like she can read my shift in focus.

I don't think there's anything this woman could say right now that could make me leave. She's obviously gorgeous. Her skin is smooth like a peach and she has a freckle to the side of her mouth I want to lick off. And her lips? They're full and ripe and luscious and... she's every fantasy come to life.

But her openness? That's why I'm not walking away. Her openness is a hook. And I'm the fish.

I've had enough of talking. I take off my jacket and throw it on the couch.

"You want a drink?" she asks and flips on a light switch.

I shake my head, flip the light switch back off and stalk over to her. She starts to step backwards, and I keep walking until she's backed against the pillar to one side of the gigantic window.

Her laugh makes the muscles in my jaw tense, while the softness in her eyes makes me want to do Very. Dirty. Things.

It's been longer than I like to think about since I've gotten laid. It doesn't help that I'm stuck in the hotel for the moment, and I don't want them knowing my business or who I'm fucking. I'm beginning to learn that hotel staff gossip, and I don't like anyone gossiping about me, regardless of the name I'm using.

I dip down and sweep my lips across hers. Her fingers press against my jaw, and I feel my body start to take over my brain. Sex is a way of switching off—the ultimate relaxation and exactly what I need. To stop thinking. Just for an hour. Or two.

I lift her leg up over my hip and slide my hand down and under and between. All that's standing between me and soft warm pussy is denim.

I bet she's wet already.

Her breathing is shallow and her breasts push against my chest as she tries to breathe more deeply.

I reach for the hem of her t-shirt and pull it off in one swift movement. I just have to have more of her. Maybe it's the accent or the way her skin seems to glow. Maybe it was the way she was trying to be kind to the scrawny bartender who was being a dick about giving her the fucking pretentious flashlight in the barely lit bar. They need lights so people can read the fucking menu, so people can fucking order. People should never feel awkward spending more money.

Am I the only person in New York with a business brain? Sometimes it feels that way.

Leo might be right—staying at the hotel might give me a

competitive advantage. But I don't want to think about that right now.

The half-naked woman in front of me is mine for tonight. That's what I need to focus on.

I snap her bra clasp open and cup her breasts, rubbing a thumb over each nipple. Her breasts are bigger than I normally go for but they're tight, nipples jutting out like they're desperate for someone to pay them a little attention. She's young.

Fuck. How young?

"Where did you go to college?" I hold my hands away from her like she's pointing a gun at me.

The expression of bliss on her face gives way to a frown. "What?"

"College?" I snap. "Where did you go?" There's no way I'm getting myself into the mess of fucking someone underage.

"Exeter. In England. Why?"

Fuck, I don't know anything about English colleges. Exeter? Is that made up?

"You graduated?" I ask.

"Is this a job interview?" she asks. "You're either going to put your hands on me or you're going to have to leave. I don't want a job. Not from you, anyway."

For a split second, I want to ask her who she wants a job from. Most people would *pay me* to work for me. And then she reaches her hand to my crotch, and I come back to my senses.

I grab her wrist and pin it to the column above. I press a kiss to her neck. "How old are you?" I growl against her skin. She smells of peaches and something darker. Something older.

"Twenty-one," she pants. Her hips lift away from the column and press against me. "Does it matter?"

I hesitate and wonder if I should ask for ID, but she pushes me away and slides down her jeans.

I'm fucking gone.

This woman's body is incredible. Soft and curvy. The glow coming in from the city light it up like she's a fucking painting. Every curve and mound. Everything about her is sexy.

"You have a beautiful body," I say.

She nods. "Right." She pushes out a hip and puts a hand on it. "And it's just going to waste right now. So... you need to do your thing."

I huff out a laugh. She's got a point. I need to stop fucking around and start fucking *her*.

I undo my shirt buttons and strip down until we're facing each other naked. It's an unfair trade. She can see I'm hard. But I don't know exactly how wet she is.

I take two steps toward her, lift her leg over my hip again. This time there's no denim in the way and I can sink my fingers into her. We both exhale at the same time, deriving pleasure from the same thing. Feeling. Sensation. Anticipation.

My brain begins to unlock, like I needed this. Her. To enable myself to let go a little. I smooth my fingers along her folds and she starts to writhe. She has no idea how good tonight is going to get.

She starts to reach for me, but that's not how this is going to go. Like most things, sex is about layers, and layer one is about finding out how she works. What makes her sigh. What makes her scream. What makes her sing.

I push deeper, all the while not taking my gaze from hers. Her eyes flit around as if she's looking for an explanation to go along with the feelings in her body. She doesn't need to make it so complicated. It's right in front of her.

It's me.

I'm doing that to you.

I'm making you feel that good. That quickly. That deeply.

I bring my other hand to her nipple and pinch. And she comes, juddering on my fingers.

That was easy.

"What the fuck was that?" she asks breathlessly, her hands holding my shoulders, keeping herself upright.

I raise my eyebrows and smirk. I expect her to elaborate, but she just looks at me expectantly.

I sink to my knees. There's nothing better than a face full of pussy. I've heard there are guys who never go down on women. Who the fuck are they and why the fuck not?

"Bennett," she cries as I grab her ass, keeping her steady as I explore her with my mouth.

Christ this feels good. Like... coming home or something.

I work my tongue between her folds, but she's struggling to stay upright. Her first orgasm has left her weak. Maybe I should have given her a few minutes to recover. I guide her down to the floor, open her legs, and resume my feast. She tastes sweet and hot, and her symphony of moans and cries urge me on. It's like she has some kind of dopamine gun and she's shooting me full of the stuff.

Sex is all about gratification. But the woman under me seems to promise more than that. It's like there's gold in there and I'm searching for it. There's something about her that makes me want more.

"Bennett," she cries out again, and I pause to look up at her as she comes. Again.

I shift, pressing kisses up from her pussy.

She whispers something but I don't catch it.

"Get off!" she screams.

I freeze, and then pull away. "Are you okay?"

"I'm not sure," she says, as she lifts her arms above her head. "I'm really not sure. All I know is you have to keep away from me. At least let me recover before you touch me again. I don't know what the hell you're doing, but it's powerful magic that you have and I need to regain my strength."

I laugh. This woman is so... different.

I stand, bend, and scoop her up, ignoring her yelping. Glancing around, I see the door to what I presume is a bedroom and head there. It can't be comfortable lying on the floor. She'll recover more quickly if she's comfortable.

She sighs as I lay her down. I double back and go get water for us both.

"Bring condoms," she calls out.

I chuckle at her request.

"Here," I say, offering her one of the glasses of water.

"Did you bring condoms?"

I hold up my wallet. "But take your time. I wouldn't want you to overexert yourself."

"How old are you?" she asks. She sits up, and I try not to look at the sway of her breasts because I'm already as hard as it's possible to be. I don't need additional encouragement.

"Thirty-four," I reply, shifting to sit against the headboard.

"Maybe magic comes with age." Her eyes slice to my wallet on the bedside table and then back to meet mine.

Carefully, she places her hands on my arms and straddles me. "Hey," she says.

"Hey," I reply.

"I think you're really handsome."

I get that tug, deep inside me again.

"I think you're really beautiful."

A shy smile uncurls on her face. She presses her finger-tips into my skin, over my collarbones, up my neck and over my jaw, almost like she's modeling me out of clay, putting her finishing touches to her creation.

Tentatively she leans forward and places a kiss on my lips. Something tells me she wants to lead this. I try to tamp down the urge to take over and set the pace. She shifts her body closer to mine and her hand comes up to hold my face. My lips open to let in her warm tongue, and as mine meets hers, the growl I've been holding back escapes. She gasps and pulls back.

She sighs. "Thank god. I thought you might actually be able to make me come from that sound alone."

I grin and cup her face, leaning forward for a follow-up kiss. It somehow feels chaste and intimate and... unusual to be in bed like this, talking and kissing.

"I need you to be careful with me," she says, looking at me. She reaches for my wallet, but I get to it before she does. I don't want her seeing my full name anywhere. I take out one of the condoms and hand it to her.

"Careful?" I ask.

She takes a breath, and I feel her body lift from where it's connected to mine. "I just think you could break me." She's not joking. There's no humor to her voice. She hands me back the condom.

"I'll be careful," I reply.

I put the condom on and she moves away and lies back on the bed, nudging me with her knee. The expression on her face is so innocent. So tentative. It unleashes some kind of protectiveness or possessiveness in me.

As I move over her, our bodies slide together like they're locking into place, like she's opening herself up and it's because of me. I push into her, carefully, slowly, for her and also for me. I need to take this slow. She's so concentrated that I might overdose on her if I don't proceed with caution.

I dip and press a kiss to her neck and I feel her exhale. "You feel so perfect," I whisper. She's tight and soft and warm, and I want the next five seconds to play on a loop for the next year.

"Bennett," she cries out, her fingernails sinking into my shoulders. If feels good to hear my name from her mouth. Too good. I start to move and immediately my skin goes hot.

"I'm going to try really—" She stops as I plow into her. "I'm going to try really hard not to come."

That's what she's worried about?

"I want you to come," I growl. "And then I want you to come again."

She whimpers underneath me.

"You don't need to worry. About anything," I assure her. "I'm here."

She freezes, and then starts to shake as she comes again. I don't know if it was my words that pushed her over the edge, but it feels powerful to be able to make her feel good and safe at the same time.

"I'm sorry," she says.

At least I won't feel bad when I last less than ten minutes fucking her. It's not normally a problem I have but there's nothing normal about tonight.

I thrust into her. "Don't ever apologize. Making you come..."

I can't finish the end of my sentence. Because what would I say? Making you come feels powerful, feels right, feels like something I've never experienced before. I can't say any of that because it's cheesy as fuck. I met this woman a couple of hours ago.

These feelings are obviously because I've gone too long without a naked woman underneath me. Which means none of what's in my head better make its way out of my mouth.

She wraps her legs around me, the change of angle making me clench my jaw and fist my hands. Her palms leave a trail of heat in their wake as she brings them down my chest. She circles her fingers around the base of me and squeezes as I withdraw.

Fuuuck.

"Do that again and I'll be the one coming," I growl out.

A smile pulls at the corners of her mouth and she doesn't move her hand.

Two can play at that game. I dip my head and take a nipple into my mouth. I suck and then graze it with my teeth.

She pulls in a breath, arching her back, pressing our bodies closer, tighter.

She thought she was done for the night.

She was wrong.

I push faster, my vision blurry, my body soaked in the feel of her. It's the closest I've ever been to heaven.

"Bennett."

I feel her begin to tighten around me, and I know I'm not going to survive it. It's too much. She's too much. Too good. Too...

My orgasm barrels up my spine like it's chasing hers. And I explode into her.

FOUR

Efa

As I make my way down to the basement, the people coming up the stairs don't even meet my eye, let alone look up to greet me. I can feel the stress in the air. I can't help but wonder if it's always like this. Maybe the lack of sleep last night is making me paranoid and I'm just imagining things.

I was supposed to meet Gretal in her office on the ground floor, but when I got there, someone directed me to the basement.

I glance around and through an internal window, where there's a meeting taking place. Going by the uniforms, it looks like the housekeeping staff is gathered.

Someone pops their head out the door. "Are you Eddie?"

Hearing my name, the name everyone has called me without exception for a very long time, makes an image of Bennett flash in my brain. Specifically, how his lips curled around the name I was born with.

I shake myself out of the half-second trance and nod. "Yes. I'm looking for Gretal."

"I'm Gretal. Come in. I'm going to put you in house-keeping for the first couple of days. There's been a bit of a bug going around, so we're short-staffed. Join us."

Gretal is British and instantly I feel a little more at home. She holds the door open and I stand against the wall, listening to the person at the head of the room.

"It's going to be a tough day. But we're fucking New Yorkers. We eat tough for breakfast."

Frankly, I could do without a tough day. Last night was the kind I need two days to recover from. Approximately. I don't know exactly because I've never experienced anything like it. Bennett was attractive, attentive, and had a dick that should be certified dangerous, but it wasn't just that. He seemed to *know* my body. Maybe he just got it because he was older. Maybe Americans are just better at sex. Or maybe Bennett is a witch.

I'm ticking the box that says "all of the above," because I still feel him in every muscle in my body, in the oval bruises on my hips where he tried to hold me still as I writhed beneath him. I still feel him in the chafed skin of my thighs from his stubble as he worked his tongue so expertly. Again and again.

Last night was a revelation and I need processing time. Hell, I need recovery time.

Someone groans, pulling me back to the moment. The woman at the front talking points her finger at the groaner. "Don't you dare go down. I need you."

It feels like I'm in a football locker room, not next to three industrial washing machines in the basement of a New York hotel.

"We'll do this. And then we'll do it again tomorrow."

Gretal steps forward. "Thank you in advance for all your hard work. I'm going to do my best to get agency staff and draft in other members of the hotel." She puts her hand on my shoulder. "Eddie's the first newbie of the day. More to follow."

There's a whooping from someone in the audience, and I can't tell if it's for me or the idea that more hands on deck have been promised.

The meeting breaks up and people start to move around.

"It's going to be a bit of a baptism of fire," Gretal says, turning to me. "Best way to learn in my experience. Plus we don't have a choice. There's been a vomiting bug passing through the housekeeping staff, which means we're under-staffed by thirty percent. There's a lot to do, but you won't be on your own. You're going to be working with Marcella. She's our longest-serving housekeeper and works exclusively on the suites. If you can work on suites, you can work anywhere. It's a good training ground. You up for it?" She doesn't wait for a response, just waves over her shoulder and shouts, "Marcella, this is Eddie. Come say hi."

I'm not going to mention that up until the age of sixteen, we had housekeepers that did all our cleaning. I'm just going to get stuck in.

"I'm up for it," I say decisively, even though I get the impression neither Marcella nor Gretal have time to give a shit. Which is fair enough. Everyone is clearly in panic mode.

"That's the spirit," Gretal says. "You'll be here for the week. At least. Marcella will deal with your hours and uniform. Any questions, you know where I am."

I nod, silently terrified about what I've let myself in for. A summer job sounded like a great idea. A summer job in New York sounded even better. Now that I'm in the basement of this hotel, I'm starting to get homesick.

"Hey," says a tiny woman with very white teeth, her black hair tied back in a bun. She pulls a trolley behind her. "Come and I'll show you how to stock a cart. Grab that one." She indicates to a black, open-shelved trolley up against the wall. "It's Debbie's but she won't be in this week."

I go ahead and maneuver the trolley toward Marcella as everyone disperses.

"This is the room that stocks everything non-food," she says.

Marcella's not going to want to tell me anything twice, so I pull up my phone and start making notes.

"I always start with towels, because it's a pain in the ass to be short on towels. We've been running out of bath mats lately, so be sure to grab those first."

I type furiously.

"These are bath towels—not to be confused with bath mats," she says. "Five in a pack," she says, picking up a stack of towels wrapped in plastic. "We do suites, but don't be fooled thinking we're going to need fewer towels. The people in the suites like a *lot* of extra towels."

She rips through the plastic and starts stacking towels on the bottom shelf of the trolley. I copy her. We do the same with hand towels and bath mats. "Some girls stack their carts the night before." She winces. "Things tend to go missing overnight, and then you're stuck going through the whole process all over again the next day. Better to wait for the morning."

"The other housekeepers take stuff?"

She nods. "It's usually only agency staff and the evening staff that do it—the lazy ones. There's a core eight of us that would never act like that to each other, but..." She shrugs. "It's dog-eat-dog in this business."

Dog-eat-dog? What are we doing, mixed martial arts or making beds?

She shows me to the cabinet with the toiletries. "Make sure your refill cans are topped up. It's a pain in the ass having to top up the shampoo and conditioner and shower gel and not just replace the disposable bottles, but that's what you get when you treat the planet like shit. If you see one of these..." She holds up a white, plastic funnel that seems like it's attached to a chain she wears around her waist. "Grab it and don't let it go. They're like gold dust. I take this little fucker home with me or it would be gone in an instant." She snaps her fingers. "Without it, half the shampoo ends up in the bath and you end up spending too long cleaning it off and going to get more refills."

I surreptitiously scan the area for a funnel, but the room is so full with stuff, I can't see anything other than color.

"I can send you a link on Amazon," she says.

"Oh, you bought your own?" I ask.

She just shrugs.

We finish stocking our trollies, which I actually quite enjoy, making room for everything like a giant jigsaw. We double-check we have all the cleaning supplies we need, then head toward the lifts.

"Second rule of housekeeping, after restocking the towels first, is always use the service elevators. You'll get fired if anyone sees you using a guest elevator. But the service elevators are always next to the guest elevators through the door opposite, so you can still follow the signs."

"Okay, good tip."

Out of the elevators, I follow Marcella along a corridor. "If we can get into these two suites at the same time, it saves us from having to go down to the basement and across to the other elevators. Saves so much time. But... third rule is, do whatever you can to service the rooms when the guest is out."

"Okay, isn't that always the case?"

She sucks in a breath like I have too much to learn for this lifetime. "Absolutely not. Especially in the suites. Some of them are used just like someone's home. They're not necessarily out at work or sightseeing all day. But if the guest is in-room, it's the worst. First off, they always remember a thousand more things they want: extra face-cloths, more tissues, a blanket or a different type of pillow. Plus they watch how you do things and the number of complaints you get is ridiculous. People have very firm views on how long the vacuum should be running." She rolls her eyes. "The upside is that the tips go up when guests can put a face to the person cleaning up their shit. Literally, in some cases."

"Oh, well, that's good," I say.

"It's the *only* good thing about it. If you can, avoid it. Especially if you're new."

We arrive at a hotel door and she flashes me a smile. "This"—she points at the light by the door that glows orange —"this is what you're looking for. They've pressed 'make up the room'—that means they're out and they want their room done ASAP." She presses the buzzer next to the sign. "Always ring the bell, even when they've put the sign on. You never know what you might walk in on. Last year, Trudy walked in on a man naked, writing all over himself with a Sharpie."

"Was it a performance art project or something?"

There's no answer, so she slips out a key and lets us in. "Who knows. But nobody's mental health needs to see shit like that. Always knock."

She tucks her plastic key into her apron pocket. "Carts always stay outside. This guest is on his own, so it's a relatively easy clean. Can you start by emptying the trash cans? I'll bring out the used towels."

"Sure," I say. We both get to work. The suite is beautiful. There's a living room with a large L-shaped sofa opposite a big-screen TV with stunning views toward the park. There's a bar at one end, a desk at the other, and a door leading through to a dining room, complete with eight chairs. I empty the rubbish and line the bins with fresh bags, while Marcella moves the dirty towels out of the bathroom and then comes into the bedroom to strip the beds of their sheets.

"Let's make the bed," she says. "We need yellow sheets."

That didn't sound right, but I follow her to the trolley.

"You see?" She points to some yellow stitching at the edge of the sheets. "The reds are small doubles. The yellows are kings. We use mainly yellows."

We set to work and Marcella patiently teaches me how to make the bed—something I thought was a simple task I'd been doing for years, but apparently not as a professional.

"You prefer people traveling on their own?" I ask, trying to make conversation.

"Yes, and for business. Those people tend to be tidy and are out a lot, so there's no problem getting in there to service the room. They don't tip as well, but that's okay. I prefer an easy life."

"How long do people stay?"

"Usually only a couple of days. But the guy in here has been here almost a week and there's no sign of him leaving. Apparently, he's booked in for a month."

"A month? How come?"

"Who knows. Maybe his apartment is flooded? Has roaches? But we don't get many people here in that scenario because the insurers won't pay the room rates. Especially the suites. So I don't know this guy's deal. Maybe he cheated on his wife and she's kicked him out."

We finish making the bed and Marcella shows me how to reset the room—how the remote control must go in the same place, how we have to check the notepads have paper and any guest charger wires or computer cables are secured in neat loops with a hotel-branded cable tidy. Everywhere is dusted, curtains are pulled to exactly the same distance each side, cushions are plumped and put back in a specific order only Marcella seems to know. Tables are tidied and the fruit bowl taken away.

I open the wardrobe doors to put back a discarded coat hanger. Dark suits fill the space on one side, bright white shirts on the other. I slot in the additional hanger to the end of the row and trail my hands over the suit jackets. Someone has expensive taste. I get a whiff of a familiar scent I can't place. It smells rich and dark and sexy. My mind is still so full of Bennett, I can't imagine who else would smell like this. I shake my head, trying to clear my mind of images of the night before, and close the wardrobe door.

Marcella works like lightning. She's done three things by the time I get to the end of a question about my one job.

We're almost finished in the bathroom when Marcella comes in with additional loo roll. "The other suite on this level—the Avenue—has just put their light on. The only thing left in here is the mirrors. Can I leave you in here to do that and I'll make a start down the hall?"

She must see the panic in my face. The mirrors run all along the vanity unit behind the two sinks and on the backs of the doors. I've never cared whether mine at home are perfectly clean, as long as I can see through them.

"Don't worry, I'll come back and check them."

"I'll do my best," I say.

"Okay, I've cleared out all our things and I'm going to move the carts so they're by the Avenue Suite. Just come to me when you're done." She hands me two cloths and a bottle of what I hope is miracle glass cleaner.

I set to work, determined to do a good job. Training me must be additional work Marcella really didn't need today, and she already works really hard. I don't want her to have to redo the mirrors in here. I need to lighten her load a little.

I'm a few minutes into my transformation of the mirrors when I hear the door to the suite open. Shit, I really wanted to be finished before she came back. She's probably finished the Avenue Suite by now and I haven't even managed to clean some mirrors.

She must have forgotten something because she doesn't come in right away. That gives me an extra few seconds to finish things off.

I'm polishing the mirror on the back of the door when something behind me catches my eye. There's a smear behind the left sink. I spin, determined to get it before Marcella walks in. I reach it just as the double doors to the bathroom open.

I glance up expecting Marcella in the reflection, but it's not her I see.

The room sways, but I manage to spin until I'm face-to-face with... Bennett.

I reach for the marble counter to steady myself. I glance down to find he's bare-chested. He's only wearing shorts, and even though I've seen him in less, it takes me a minute to get my breath.

I know what that chest feels like. I know what those hands can do. I know how his mouth tastes.

"What the fuck are you doing in my bathroom?" he yells, pulling me out of the vortex of memories from last night.

His bathroom?

His tone takes me by surprise. Last night he seemed to be the kind of guy who wouldn't be fazed by anything or anyone. Like he could stand, with his hands in his pockets, and wouldn't move if a hurricane passed through. Yet me cleaning his bathroom is getting him riled.

"Cleaning your mirror, dickwad. What does it look like I'm doing?"

Shit. I probably shouldn't have said that, given he's a guest.

He takes a couple of steps toward me and I have to move back, so I'm half-lying on the sinks. His eyes are narrowed and suspicious, his mouth taut. He's seething. "What are you really doing here? How did you know this was my room?"

I push his chest and dip under his arm to get away. "Stop being an asshole. I'm cleaning your bathroom. And now I'm done, so goodbye." I turn, scurry out of the bathroom and fling open the door to the suite. Marcella is two steps away, and she must see the panic in my eyes.

Her gaze darts behind me, and I realize Bennett is following me.

"Who are you?" he thunders.

"I'm so sorry, Mr. Fordham," Marcella says. "Eddie here is new. We were just finishing your suite. We're all done."

I don't turn to see his expression. I just walk briskly towards the trollies outside the Avenue Suite, determined to hide the tremor in my hands.

FIVE

Bennett

I scroll through emails on my phone as I stand with my back against the door to "Efa's" apartment. I don't expect her to appear, but if there's the slightest chance, I'm not going to pass up the opportunity to confront her. I have to know who she's working for.

I'm furious that my team hasn't managed to find a connection between Efa or Eddie Cadogan, the woman I fucked last night, and any tech company. She's good at what she does. So far, everything she told me checks out. I remembered she said she went to Exeter University in the UK, which the team confirmed. They've even tracked the owner of this apartment—Vincent Cove, the cousin of Eddie's sister's fiancé. I'm pretty certain she said he was her brother-in-law, but it's close enough not to matter.

Vincent Cove doesn't have much of a connection to tech. He has his fingers in a lot of pies, but there's no obvious connection between him and anything Fort Inc. is doing. I just can't connect the dots.

The elevator's doors rattle, then open, and I stand up straight, hoping Efa's got the nerve to show.

To my surprise, she rounds the corner.

She sees me and rolls her eyes. "What have I done to deserve this?" she asks. "If you get me fired, I'm going to lose it. A friend of a friend of my brother-in-law got me this job, and I don't want to fuck it up."

I snort. She's still continuing with this made-up story. "Another brother-in-law. Yeah, right. Why don't you tell me who you're working for and they can be the subject of my ire instead of you?"

"Ire? How old are you exactly, Grandad?"

"A decent vocabulary isn't exclusive to older generations." What am I doing? I don't need an argument about semantics. I want answers. "Tell me who you're working for."

She digs around in her purse and pulls out a set of keys. "If I have to, I'll call the police. Move out of my way."

"Efa, just tell me who you're working for." I deliberately block her path.

"Gretal!" she shouts. "She manages The Avenue. That's my boss."

"Shut up!" someone shouts from somewhere behind a wall. Our argument is clearly being overheard.

I step forward so I don't have to raise my voice and instantly regret it, because I can smell peaches. Memories from our night together flash through my brain like a slideshow. I close my eyes and will them away. I need to focus on extracting information, not reliving my manipulation.

"Stop lying to me," I bite out as quietly as I can. "It makes no sense that you'd be staying in an apartment like this and working as a housekeeper. It doesn't add up."

She gives a one-shouldered shrug. "So?" she whispers.

"Make it make sense," I urge, trying to keep my voice as low as possible, while at the same time, fighting the urge to trail my fingers over her cheek and down her neck.

Her eyes flicker from my eyes to my lips, like she's having the same filthy thoughts I am. "Why?" she mumbles. "I don't owe you anything."

Her words snap me out of my trance.

"You're a liar," I hiss into her ear and turn to leave. She's right that I can't make her explain herself. It's absolutely infuriating. I'll get one of my team to surveil her. There's nothing she can do, no one she can call, without me knowing about it from now on.

"I haven't lied about anything," she calls after me, risking the wrath of her neighbor. "I'm working here for the summer. Just because my family is rich and has a fancy apartment doesn't make me a liar."

I stop and stalk back to her. I don't need to attract any more attention to myself at the moment. "So why didn't you tell me you were working in the hotel?" I whisper-shout.

"Why didn't you tell me you were *staying* in the hotel? Did you want to get into my flat for some reason? What are *you* hiding?" She steps forward and jabs her finger into my chest. I glance down and she withdraws her hand. I've never hate-fucked a woman before, but I'm starting to understand the appeal.

The fact is, I'm staying at the hotel because I *am* hiding. So why didn't she tell me she was working there?

"We're not talking about me." My voice is low, but I'm not whispering.

"*I* am. Why would you want to waste time going to my place when we could have taken the lift to yours?" She transfers her weight from hip to hip, and I try not to notice the way her entire body moves so gracefully. "Make *that* make sense! Maybe you hang out at the hotel bar every night and pick up a different woman, and maybe it feels kinda icky to be fucking three thousand different women in the same bed."

"Or maybe I just want to leave when I want," I rally. "There are a thousand reasons to want to go to your place."

"The thing is, I don't really care. You didn't tell me about the hotel room. So what? I didn't tell you that today I'm due to start a summer job at the hotel—"

"Not just a summer job. A summer job servicing *my* room."

She gasps in exasperation. "I had no idea which department I would be working in. You think I personally passed around a vomiting bug to the housekeeping staff so they'd be short-staffed, guaranteeing I'd be assigned to fill the gaps? Then—what? I used my mind control techniques to make sure I was assigned your room? Have you heard yourself? You need a therapist. Or a holiday. Or both."

I push my hands through my hair, exasperated at the way she has an answer for everything. "Why on earth do you need to do housekeeping at The Avenue when your family clearly has money?"

She puts her hand on her hip like I've just asked her a personal question I had no right to. She's not wrong. "First, it's none of your business. Second, *I* don't have money. Not yet. Thirdly, my brother-in-law—or my sister's brother-in-law? I keep meaning to find out if that makes him my brother-in-law or not. Anyway, Nathan used to work with Gretal, the manager of The Avenue, and he put us in touch. I wanted to have some fun this summer. I just graduated. Wanted a job I didn't have to think too much about so I could keep myself busy and... you know... hang out in New York." Her voice starts to rise as she speaks and someone starts banging on the wall. Do they know they're in New York City and not Connecticut? I might have to buy this building and evict whoever it is for being an asshole. "I figured there are other opportunities here too. I'm just figuring shit out. I'm twenty-one. I'm allowed to be figuring stuff out."

I sigh. I'm a good people reader. I can sniff out a charlatan, a liar, a cheat a thousand miles away. Efa isn't who I've accused her of being.

"So it's coincidence that you turned up in my hotel suite today?" I ask, my voice returning to normal. It's not a question. I'm sure she's telling the truth. It's just a *hell* of a coincidence.

"New York's a small place, I guess. But is it? Because I was there last night checking things out before I started work. You were at the hotel bar where you were staying... picking up chicks to bang. It's not that big of a coincidence."

I groan. "I wasn't there to pick up chicks. Do people even say 'chicks' anymore?"

"Fine. *A chick.* To bang. If you want to be pedantic."

This is an argument I have no interest in winning. She doesn't need to know that I haven't picked up "a chick" in a while.

"Coincidence," I say, more resolutely this time.

"Right," she says, her eyes widening. "So this is the bit where you apologize for acting like a dickwad."

I want to raise an issue with the use of the term *dickwad*, but I have a feeling now's not the time. "Yeah," I say. "Look, I'm sorry if I jumped to conclusions."

She rolls her eyes. "Very poor apologizing. You're sorry

if you jumped to conclusions? You *definitely* jumped to conclusions. And on top of that, you've maligned my character, been rude and aggressive and"—she lowers her voice again—"not nice."

I pull in a breath. She's not wrong. I also want to congratulate her on her use of the word *maligned*. She's proved me right that a good vocabulary isn't the preserve of a man in his thirties, but I have a feeling she won't take that well, either. I've already been enough of an asshole without adding condescension to the mix.

"I'm sorry I jumped to conclusions and I've been rude, and aggressive and... what was it? Oh, yes—not nice." Although it was the least offensive thing she accused me of, it's the part that sticks in my gut. Call me an asshole and I can brush it off, but somehow, *not nice* feels like a bigger deal. Maybe I'm going soft in my old age. Or maybe it's because this woman... last night was so... intense.

"Better," she says. "That sounded more like an apology."

"Enjoy your evening," I say with a nod. It's not like I'm expecting to get invited in. Not after the exchange we just had. But if she did ask me in, I'm not sure I could say no.

The click and snap of a door being opened catches my attention, and I whip my head around.

A woman with orange hair tied up with a headscarf puts her head out of the door. "Can you two lovebirds have your argument in your apartment? I'm trying to work in here." I'm not sure if I imagine it, but a squawking sound comes from behind her. It sounds like an exotic bird. "You see?" she says accusatorily before slamming the door without waiting for our answer.

I turn back to Efa and raise my eyebrows.

"And now you got me in trouble with my neighbors. Be

gone." She sweeps her hands up in dismissal, like I'm completely inconsequential to her. I can't remember anyone ever treating me that way. Then again, Efa is proving unique in more ways than one.

"See you around, knowing my good luck," she says.

I let out a chuckle and head to the elevators.

SIX

Efa

My hands shake as I unlock the door of the Park Suite. Obviously, I didn't tell Marcella that Bennett and I knew each other. In the biblical sense. Still, she knows I'm nervous.

"You didn't do anything wrong," Marcella says. She thinks I'm shaking because I'm concerned Bennett will be inside. And I *am* nervous, but it's not nerves making me shake. It's the memories of hours of nakedness with him, and the half-dozen orgasms he wrung out of me. Then there's the way that even when he's being a total arsehole and accusing me of things that are completely and utterly not true, my entire body kinda buzzes when he's close.

I didn't expect to see him again and now I'm going to be disappointed if I don't. "He just got a shock, that's all. But if he'd checked, he would have seen the tag on the door." She hangs a sign on the door handle that, from a distance, looks like a Do Not Disturb sign, but actually says housekeeping is servicing your room.

I don't make the point that I'm ninety-nine point nine percent certain there was no such notice on Bennett's door. I get the impression that Marcella is just as concerned as me about Bennett filing a complaint against us.

"But we'll keep the carts outside the room this time, just so he's clear. And we're later today. He's probably gone to his offices or got a meeting somewhere."

I try to remember if he told me what he does for a living, but nothing springs to mind.

"I'll start on the bathroom. You start in the living room, then we'll do the bed together," she says.

I head into the living room and start to empty the bins. There's nothing in there but a beer bottle and a flyer for an off-Broadway show he must have been given on the street. Not that I'm deliberately searching his rubbish.

I'm just curious about him. He fucks like a champ, but he's paranoid as all holy hell.

He's so intense in everything he does. The way he picked me up at the bar. The way he fucks. The way he talks. The way he argues. He's annoying but fascinating. I can't help but be interested.

The bins provide no further clue about who Bennett is or what he's doing at the hotel. Is he in town for a conference? Where does he live? His surname must be around here somewhere. I can Google him when I find it.

I straighten the cushions and find a computer mouse between the seats. I set it on the coffee table in front of the sofa. There's a charger plugged in by the floor lamp, so I pull it out and wind the cord around my hand, while taking a surreptitious look at what's been left on the table. There's a receipt for four hundred and something dollars from a restaurant. Wow. That must have been a great meal. And one for Duane Reade. I look more closely. For condoms.

My stomach swoops and I check the date. It's for yesterday. The time is just after he left my apartment. Was he restocking? Did he have a date yesterday evening?

"Is it bad in there?" Marcella calls from the bathroom. I drop the receipt and straighten the magazines laid out on the table.

"Not really. Just tying up some cables and straightening the cushions. In there?"

"No, this guy is OCD. All his toiletries are in a straight line. He might actually be a serial killer. Did you see how good-looking he was? And the body on him? Nothing good can come from that."

Oh, Marcella, how wrong you are.

"I'm going to dust," I call out.

"Okay, do the bedroom as well."

I look for clues about Bennett on every surface I shine. But other than those two receipts, I find nothing. There are no papers lying about. No loose change by the bed or night-time reading.

I pull open a drawer to find neatly organized socks and boxer briefs. I can't resist, pulling out a pair of his pants and holding them up. They're roomy. Which is necessary for him. That guy has a lot to contain. But there's nothing else hiding amongst the underwear.

The next drawer is equally unhelpful, with neat stacks of dark-colored gym gear and nothing else. What am I expecting to find? His diary, complete with a small gold lock keeping the pages secure?

Next up is the wardrobe. I open the door and am hit with the familiar smell of him again. I drink it in, and I feel it on my body like his hands gliding over my skin, down my throat and down, down, down.

I flick through the jackets, surreptitiously dipping my

fingers into pockets, but there's nothing here to tell me anything other than the size he wears. And I already knew that.

Is it normal to leave no clues about who you are in a hotel room?

Is he hiding something?

Or everything? I really don't know anything about him other than his first name.

I pop my head into the bathroom, looking for clues. "Do you need help in here?" I ask.

"No, I'm nearly done. Can you strip the bed and start on the pillowcases? I'll come in when I can."

I glance around while Marcella's talking. As she said, there are limited toiletries on the vanity unit, all neatly set out in a row. There's a brown leather bag on the corner of the bath, and although there's probably nothing in it, I wonder if there's a way I could check. Maybe Marcella will ask me to do the mirrors again and I'll get a chance to see if Bennett is a man or a robot.

"No problem," I reply and head out to the trolley. I swap my duster for pillowcases and sheets and move through to the bedroom. I start with the pillowcases. They smell like him. Not that I'm a weirdo, deliberately sniffing an almost-stranger's pillowcase—I just can't help but notice. I didn't see any aftershave in the bathroom, so I'm left wondering what gives him that unique scent. It doesn't smell like it came out of a bottle. It smells like his skin, when he was over me, pushing into me, straining like he was struggling to hold back.

"How you doing?" Marcella asks from behind me. I jump at her being there, like I'm guilty of something—fantasizing about my one-night stand.

"Yeah, just stripping off the old sheets."

The sound of the door to the suite opening catches our attention and we both freeze, looking at each other.

There's definitely someone in the living room, but I'm not about to investigate. "You wait here, I'll go and get... something."

Before I can try to convince her not to go anywhere, Marcella has headed out.

"Good morning, sir," she says. "We're almost done."

I stay as still as possible, waiting for him to respond.

But I don't hear him say anything.

When Marcella returns, she's carrying bottles of water to place by the bed.

Just as she finishes setting out the water, her radio bleeps. It only went off once yesterday and it meant we had to drop everything and head to another suite to service it immediately. "This will be the Avenue Suite again." She lowers her voice to a near-whisper and continues, "He seems fine today. You finish the bed here and meet me in Avenue. Okay?"

I nod, suddenly aware of the pulse in my wrists beating against my skin.

Me and Bennett. In this room. Alone.

Bennett. Mysterious. Paranoid. But why? Who is he?

As quickly as I can, I smooth the sheets across the bed, tuck them, and try not to picture Bennett's naked body wrapped in them. Is he a deep sleeper or restless? Does he sleep naked or in PJs?

Why am I so interested?

I'm not sure if it was the good sex or the fact he's everywhere but so distant at the same time.

Every now and then I pause, but I can't hear anything. Is he even still in the other room? Maybe he went into the dining room, a polite retreat to give me space to do my job.

I finish the bed and make sure the pillows and cushions are perfectly lined up. I round the end of the bed looking at it from all angles, making sure it's exactly how it should be. Bennett is nothing if not thorough—I know that from personal experience. Plus, I want him to think I'm good at my job, even if that job is cleaning hotel rooms. From the little I know about him, I think he appreciates someone who cares about their work, who takes pride in it. He's the opposite of slap-dash and sloppy, and I imagine a careless approach in any part of his life is abhorrent to him.

I cross my arms and admire my work. It's only a bed, but it's beautifully made. Perfect in fact. A part of me wants to slide off my knickers and slip them under his pillow.

But I don't want to get myself fired.

I'm still smiling at my idea as I exit the bedroom and lock eyes with Bennett. It's like he's been waiting for me to appear. He's sitting on the sofa, a laptop on his knees. His gaze flits back to the screen.

"Housekeeping is all finished in your suite. Anything else I can do for you... sir?"

His eyes cut back to mine, and I can't help pushing down on my bottom lip with my teeth.

We still, staring at each other for what seems like forever.

His eyes snake down my body, from my eyes, to my collarbones, my breasts, my waist, hips, legs. He maps me thoroughly before meeting my eyes again.

"Nothing, thank you," he says, and for a moment I'm confused. Then I realize what he's saying—there's nothing else he needs. From housekeeping? From me? Both, I guess.

"But I want you to know that I believe you," he says.

My heart lifts. I don't know why I care, but apparently, I do.

"Good," I say. "I was telling you the truth. I have nothing to hide." I glance around the room. "Unlike you." I shouldn't have said it. Honestly, my mouth is going to get me in real trouble one day.

But he doesn't respond, and the devil on my shoulder can't resist an extra prod. "There's nothing personal of you here at all."

"So?" he asks, his tone slightly defensive.

"So, it's like you're trying to disappear. There's no scribbled note by the side of your bed. No business papers on the coffee table. Nothing in your pockets that would give away who you are or where you go every day. It's like you're a shadow. A shadow of a man."

He raises his eyebrows. "You've gone through my pockets?"

I groan. Of course he'd pick up on the one thing I shouldn't have done. "Yeah, probably not in my job description, it's just... I slept with you the night before last and I don't know anything about you."

"We had a one-night stand. We're not planning a wedding. You don't need to know me."

"Right. It's normal to not know someone if you have a one-night stand with them, I guess. I don't have access to the rule book on that, and I don't have much experience, but I'll take your word for it. Anyway, what I'm saying is, I've cleaned your hotel room from top to bottom and I feel like I know you less than I did the night I saw you naked. Not knowing is one thing, but it's like you're purposely hiding who you are."

"Why didn't you say you did computer science in college?" he asks.

"Because—wait, how do you know I did computer science at university?"

"Why didn't you tell me, Efa?"

Him saying my name startles me. Because he's the only person who uses that name and it feels oddly... intimate. "I didn't realize you required that information," I snap. "Did you need to know my bank balance at the exact time of penetration? Can you provide a list of credentials I should prepare before my next one-night stand?"

He glares at me like he's about to toss his laptop aside and challenge me to a wrestling match, but he doesn't say anything.

"The way you expect me to be so open and honest about everything—which I have been, by the way—yet you're so private and paranoid? It's weird. Anyone would think you're Ben Fort, for goodness' sake."

His eyes widen in shock.

I gasp.

The hum of the city fills the silence between us and neither of us moves. Realization trickles into my brain.

"You *are* him!" I clasp my hand over my mouth. A feeling of being completely right settles in my gut.

"Don't be ridiculous," he barks, and if looks could kill, I would be six feet under.

Bennett. Ben. That tracks. Rumors say he's young, and even though he's an "older man" for me as a lover, he's technically young as a boss-man billionaire. If he wasn't in tech, why would he be interested in me doing computer science at university?

"Get out," he says firmly.

It's all the confirmation I need that I've stumbled across Ben Fort, reclusive billionaire and CEO of Fort Inc. One of the brightest minds of his generation. And the man I always dreamed of having as a boss.

SEVEN

Bennett

I haven't left my hotel room today. A wiser man would have checked out, gone to stay at the Mandarin Oriental. Gone to stay with Worth in his brownstone. Hired an RV and slept in that, for crying out loud.

But here I am, sitting at the desk in the living area of my suite.

Waiting.

For Efa.

I could have had my team call her yesterday and ask her to sign an NDA, but something about her tells me she'd be more likely to make a fuss if I'd had someone call her than if I left it alone. It was a gamble.

Only time will tell if it will pay off.

A knock at the door sets my pulse off to a gallop. I've pressed the light to say that I want my room serviced, but I don't know who is going to walk through that door.

The lock clicks open and a trill call of "housekeeping" follows. I can't tell if it's her and I won't turn to look. Not yet. I don't want to appear eager. Or desperate. But that's exactly how I feel.

"Sir, you had your light on. Would you like us to come back later?" a voice asks.

I turn to find an older woman, her hair up in a bun on the top of her head. I can't remember if she was the woman with Efa yesterday. "Please go ahead," I say, and then Efa appears behind her, head down, like she's trying to avoid my gaze.

I turn back to my computer.

For the first time in a long time, I don't know how to play this. Should I try to convince her I'm not Ben Fort? I'm not sure she's convincible. I saw certainty in her eyes when she said the name yesterday.

I keep working, hoping a neat solution will come to me.

As I go through a presentation I've been sent, I'm aware there are people in the suite, but I don't know who's where and I try to bury myself in my work.

I don't know how much time passes before someone passes by my desk and my gaze snags on the hem of her skirt, the curve of her leg. I don't have to trail my gaze up any higher to know it's Efa. I know those legs. I've had my hands—my mouth, my tongue—on those legs.

I continue to stare as she organizes the pillows on the sofa across the room, her back to me. As she moves, I can see the outline of her backside and remember how it felt to slide my hands across it, to press my palm into her skin as I pushed into her from behind.

Fuck. I turn back to my screen and try to concentrate.

But it's not much use.

I can hear her behind the bar.

I'm aware of her everywhere.

I turn and our eyes meet immediately. I go to speak, but

she puts a finger over her mouth and flicks her eyes toward the bathroom in warning. We're not alone.

As I turn back to my laptop, the older woman emerges and scurries over to Efa. They have a short conversation that's so quiet, I wouldn't even know they were talking if I weren't so tuned in to Efa's every movement.

Efa nods and the woman tucks something into her pocket before heading out the front door. It closes with a click.

"She's gone?" I ask.

Efa nods.

"Have you told anyone?" I ask. It's a juvenile question. If she has, she's not going to admit it.

"I want a job," she replies.

"I'm not going to get you fired," I say. Is that what she thinks of me? I'm not an asshole, despite what my friends might say.

"Not here," she says like I'm an idiot. "I want a job at —" She stops and looks over her shoulder, even though we're the only two people in this suite. "At Fort," she whispers.

"What kind of job?" I ask.

"I don't care as long as it's with you." She must see my expression of shock when she says the words. "Not *you*, you. You, because you're CEO at Fort. Let me sharpen pencils. I don't care what job. Any job. I want to learn. It's part of the reason I wanted to come to New York. I wanted to work for you—Fort, I mean."

"What if I say no?"

A crease appears between her brows. "I won't give up. I think I'd be an asset."

"What do you mean you won't give up?" I ask. Do I believe she's my stalker? No. Do I believe she's not told anyone who I am? Maybe. But that doesn't mean I trust her. Does it? I don't trust anyone.

"I mean, I'll do whatever it takes for you to give me a job."

I was afraid of this. Even if she stumbled onto my identity accidentally, and our meeting wasn't premeditated, she has all the power now.

"So you'd blackmail me?" I ask.

"What? That's not what I'm saying. I'm asking you for a job."

"And if I say no?"

She comes out from behind the bar and heads toward me. On the way, she spots something on the coffee table in front of the sofa. She stops, rubs whatever it is with the blue cloth she's holding. As she bends, I can see down the front of her uniform, her milky, soft skin that I know tastes delicious, the valley between her breasts that my tongue has traveled. I can't look away. It's like I've developed a fault and I've lost all self-control. I'm Narcissus addicted to his reflection, Icarus flying toward the sun. No matter that the woman in front of me could ruin me, I can't stop staring.

She bends lower now. She's discovered something else. Her dress rides up her thighs and I'm practically panting because I want the material to go higher. And even though I've seen it all before, I want more.

Abruptly, she stands and resumes her journey toward me.

"If you say no..." She stands before me and puts one hand on a hip. "You can't say no. Or at least, you shouldn't. I'm clever. I graduated almost top of my class. I'm discreet, as you know. I'll be a real asset. Plus, I'm British. Every organization can benefit from someone with a different accent on staff."

The last thing I need at work is this woman, distracting me just walking across the office. "Discreet?" I ask, intrigued.

"Christ on a bike, you don't need to act dumb. I know exactly who you are and we banged. I've not told a soul about either thing. And believe me, there are plenty of people who would like to know. Focus on the positive: fresh blood, new eyes. I'll be good for you."

Her words vibrate in my chest and I take a deep breath, trying to push them aside.

"We have plenty of fresh blood. What will you do if I say no?"

"I'll convince you." She glances around the room. "Look how well I clean your room. I've only been at the job for two days and look how quickly I've picked everything up. I'm the same with coding. Precise. Committed. Detail-orientated. I don't stop until everything is complete.

"And it's not just coding I'm good at. Algos are my jam. I did a module on data security too. Best of all, *I want to learn*. From the best."

"I don't sleep with my employees," I say.

"Okay, well... bummer, but we won't sleep together."

"That ship has sailed." Much to my dick's disappointment, judging by my current blood flow.

"Clean slate. We can pretend it never happened."

My eyes widen. "Really?" I ask. It's teasing. Borderline flirtatious, but I just can't help it. There's no way she's going to forget coming so often in one night. It was more than obvious that it wasn't a regular occurrence.

"I'm sure the memories will fade with time." She narrows her eyes slightly. "But if you wanted to relax the rule about not fucking the staff, I'd be happy to... keep those memories sharp."

A smile curls around her lips, and I shake my head with a small grin.

I stand so we're facing each other. "Problem is, I can't hire you, because I still want to fuck you."

What is the matter with me? I should be doing damage control. This woman should have already had correspondence with my lawyers. I'm setting myself up for a fall—which I never do, both on principle and for practicality.

"I don't see how wanting to fuck me is a problem," she replies. "The feeling is entirely mutual. But however good it was, I'll take a job over your dick."

I can't help but burst out laughing. They say the British are reserved. Not this Brit.

"I'm not hiring you."

"I'm not giving up," she says. "What if I go through the proper channels? You can put me through the recruitment process. That seems fair. If I get through, I get through. If I don't, I don't."

She doesn't know that there *isn't* a recruitment process. I do all the hiring and firing, and I go by a candidate's skill set and my gut. Most recruits are brought to me by a current member of staff.

"No," I say simply, and turn back to my computer. She sighs, and I try to ignore the way the sound slips through my veins like morphine, making my limbs weak and my mind putty.

"I'm not giving up," she says.

I don't respond.

"But I'm pissed off," she says. "You won't recruit me. And I can't sleep with you again because I know it would limit my chances even further."

She's right. It's a lose-lose for her.

And for me. I can't sleep with her, even if I'm very clear

that she's not going to work for Fort Inc. It would feel like taking advantage. And I can't sleep with her even if for some reason I could employ her, because that would be taking advantage too.

There aren't many people who would describe me as unlucky, but that's how I feel right now.

The sound of the suite door clicking catches our attention at the same time and our gazes lock, as if we're about to get caught doing something we shouldn't.

We're not doing anything to feel guilty about, though. Unfortunately.

EIGHT

Efa

In between scrolling for my next Netflix addiction, I'm trying to find out more about Ben Fort. And Fort Inc. I'm also brainstorming ideas for apps and daydreaming about a job with Bennett Fordham as my boss. I'm also overlooking Manhattan while doing all of the above. There are worse ways to spend an evening.

What I like about tech is getting under the skin. Some people like the marketing or the packaging. I like the coding and technology beneath the surface, which is another reason why I think Fort Inc. and I are so well suited. They have never taken products to the public. They know it's not where their strength lies, and they're not going to be arrogant enough to think they can do it all. They do the hard stuff—invent the technology, work out the bugs, then they sell it to Apple or Google or whoever can bring it to market. The companies everyone has heard of do the marketing and branding and make everything look pretty, while Bennett gets on and does the important work.

Having met the man behind Fort, it makes complete sense. He doesn't mess around. He has no need to prove himself. He knows what he's good at and sticks to it.

If his sharp jaw and tight, hard body weren't enough, I have to have an intellectual crush on the guy too.

A knock at the door makes me jump. The building has a doorman. No one has ever knocked on that door.

I scramble to my feet and head to the door, wondering if I should open it.

"Efa?" a familiar voice booms out. "I know you're in there. Open the door."

I roll my eyes and wrangle with the locks and catches and pull open the door to find Bennett on my doorstep, looking like he just murdered someone—or wants to murder me.

"How did you get past the doorman?"

"You really need to do something about security in this place."

"Did you bribe him?" I hold the door open for him, even though I don't have an explanation for what he's doing here. He brushes past me. I try to cover up the deep breath I take of his earthy scent. I never did discover what it is that makes him smell that way.

"No, I didn't bribe him," he replies, and I follow him into the living space. "I just told him I was coming to visit you, Efa Cadogan. Then he didn't know Efa, so I gave him that ridiculous nickname."

"Eddie isn't a ridiculous nickname," I say. "It's what everyone in my entire universe calls me."

He fixes me with a stare. "Not me."

My skin starts to vibrate. What is it with this man? I think he could make me come just looking at me.

"Well, you're difficult," I say. "Want a drink? And then you can tell me what you're here for."

"Sure, I'll have a beer."

I'm shaking my head before he's finished his sentence. "I have some questionable red wine and water. That's it."

He winces at the options, which doesn't surprise me. I'm used to wine snobs.

He picks up the bottle on the coffee table in front of the sofa. "Why?" He turns to me.

"I like to think of myself as an egalitarian when it comes to wine."

He rolls his eyes, but I know he's semi-impressed by my word choice. It's who he is.

"I'll order up a beer," he says.

"How long are you planning to be here?" I say with a laugh.

"You're right. We should get down to business."

"Funny business?" I say, pulsing my eyebrows up.

He pulls out some papers from his jacket pocket. "NDA. I need you to sign."

I snatch them from him and take a seat on the sofa. "What for? You?" I unfold the documents and scan the first page. Yeah, he doesn't want me spilling any of the top-secret info I've managed to uncover about him, like the fact he smells nice.

"I've told you, I won't tell anyone. How many of these have you given out in your life? I bet the entire population of New York has signed an NDA with you. We all know who you are, but no one's talking about it." I laugh at the idea, but Bennett's face is like stone.

"Everyone at Fort has signed, but no one knows I'm also Bennett Fordham except you. You're the only one who's ever guessed."

It's as if someone's taken the air from my lungs. I snatch a breath in. He's so earnest, like he's part terrified and part impressed I've discovered him.

"You see?" I say. "I'm one of a kind. I'd be perfect at Fort. Perceptive and clever."

"Sign the document," he says, taking a seat next to me on the sofa.

"On one condition," I reply.

"As long as it doesn't involve an orgasm."

I can't help but laugh. "I *should* refuse to sign without an orgasm. But actually, it's only a temporary fix. I think if I was going to use sex as the consideration, I'd make it an ongoing obligation. How often would be appropriate, do you think?" I curl my legs underneath me, when what I really want to do is climb into Bennett's lap.

He narrows his eyes at me in mock outrage. "I can't see how you'd find it a problem getting sex if that's what you want. You don't need anyone contractually obligated."

He's right I suppose, but what I learned from a night with Bennett is that not all sex is equal. In fact, sex with Bennett is an entirely different experience to having sex with any of my previous partners. Like taking a quick, perfunctory shower compared to swimming in the Indian Ocean at sunset after a cocktail.

"It's a matter of quality control," I say. "I know what you're capable of." I nudge his thigh with my sock-covered foot, just wanting that physical connection to him.

I don't expect him to react, so when he circles my ankle with his fingers and pulls me towards him, I'm once again startled out of a breath.

My legs bridge over his and my bottom is tucked against the side of his thigh. Our faces are inches from each other. There's just a layer of thin cotton separating me and him. I want to unbutton my top, have him lick between my breasts. Have him consume me like he did just a few nights ago. Other than a job at Fort, it's *all* I want right now.

He slides his hands up my thighs. "We've been through why this is a bad idea." His voice has that gravelly edge to it, like his stubble against my skin.

"But," I say on an exhale, tipping my chin up, as if my neck is craving his mouth just as much as the rest of me. "Have we properly considered all the reasons why it's a *good* idea?" My fingers trail against his jaw. "A *really* good idea."

He growls and I gasp.

"Efa."

He pulls away and stands, pushing his hands through his hair. "I can't think straight when you're so close."

A small smile nudges at the edges of my lips. I'm taking a victory from that. He wants me. He's fighting it, but it's an ongoing battle.

"Thinking straight is overrated," I say.

"Sign the NDA," he says.

I stand up and move toward him. It's provocative, but I can't help myself. It seems like a waste for us to be far apart in the same room, when there's no one here to catch us.

"Why should I sign it? What are you going to do if I talk? Imprison me? Sue me? All this does"—I pick up the papers—"is put a moral obligation into a legal document, but there's no real remedy if I breach it. Not one that works, because once the cat is out of the bag, there's no putting it back in."

He growls again and grabs my face, pressing his lips against mine, his tongue pushing into my mouth like he's searching for something. My hands slide up his chest and he presses up against me.

All I can feel is his hardness. His chest, his stomach. His cock.

I'm shaking with anticipation of feeling it all and more and everywhere.

He pulls at the buttons of my pajama top, not letting go of my face, holding me in place, like he just can't get enough.

I know that feeling.

I don't help him. *Won't* help him. I dig my hands into his hair, and all of a sudden, he pulls away.

"Fuck," he gasps, wiping his mouth with the back of his hand. "Fuck, Efa."

I can't think of anything to say.

"Yes, please?" I ask.

"No," he booms. "I've told you. We can't. Not now. Not when I know you want a job. It's like I'm taking advantage of you."

"But you're not," I say. "I'm not thinking that if I sleep with you, you'll hire me. It's Fort Inc., not Buy Your Discount Electricals Here Inc. You want the best. I just have to convince you that I meet your criteria. Sex has nothing to do with that."

He scrubs his hands over his face. "I can't. It doesn't matter what you say, I can't let it happen. I would feel like I've abused my position."

Gah. Why does he have to be such a stand-up guy?

"I have to leave," he says and heads to the door.

I follow him. "Then why did you come?" I ask him.

He stops, one hand on the door handle, and frowns like he thinks I've missed something. "To get you to sign the NDA."

"You could have put it in my letterbox." I fold my arms. "Handed it to me tomorrow when I change your sheets. You could have slipped it under my door. You had other options. But you didn't use any of them."

He pushes his thumb over his temple. "I wanted to make sure you signed it."

I raise my eyebrows because I haven't signed it, and he came right on in and took a seat on my sofa. "How's that working out for you?" I ask.

"Good night, Efa," he says and leaves.

I've not gotten the six orgasms I deserve, but at least I've left him frustrated as hell, in every sense of the word.

NINE

Bennett

I could be locked away in the dining room, but I'm working at the desk in the living area of my suite, determined to torture myself.

Or not.

Depending on who comes to service the suite today.

I'm acting like a three-year-old with zero self-control. What on earth am I hoping to achieve by sitting here while she cleans around me? A boner? Apart from that, nothing positive can come out of me being near her, unable to have her.

Yet here I sit.

The click of the door lock echoes in my ear like it's a mallet on a gong. Does it indicate the start of something or my impending doom?

Either. Both?

I don't look around to see if she's here today. I'm concerned that if the older woman is with her, she'll know immediately what I'm thinking. The last thing I want to do is draw attention to myself.

I try to work. I respond to emails. I try to read a report one of the technicians has sent me, but I read the first line over and over. It's like someone's coated the words in Teflon and I slide over them, unable to absorb their meaning.

I don't know how long it's been, but the room has gone quiet behind me. I'm tempted to stand, to investigate if there's anyone still here. Before I can, my eye snags on someone emerging from the bathroom. I snap my head back to the laptop before I can see who it is, but I already know. I can feel her. She's here. And it brings me peace and war in the same breath.

What is it with this woman?

Okay, we had a great night together. A fantastic night together. There was a connection beyond the physical that I'm not used to feeling. But I've built a billion-dollar company. I'm used to being able to give up the temptation of tasting the apple of today to grow the orchard of tomorrow. So why is resisting her so damn difficult?

Yes, she's beautiful. But this is New York City. Beautiful women are everywhere.

And she's smart. Like really smart—even though she says it herself. That's a turn-on, sure.

Then there's her ass, so deliciously round in contrast to her narrow waist, begging my hands to span the luscious width of it, moving her to my will.

Her long legs that draw me in, like a road I know leads only to nirvana.

And that smile that tells me she's in on the joke, but isn't about to tell me until I've told her all my secrets.

I'm so fucking done.

Unable to resist any longer, I turn around, not caring

what expression she sees on my face. She'll know I'm looking for her and her alone.

I hear something clatter to the ground in the bathroom and somebody mumble something.

Then she emerges. She wipes her hand down her apron, pulls out the duster tucked into her pocket and heads into the living area.

We lock eyes, and she grins at me like I'm the best man she's ever known. It's a smile that hits me in the chest with a smack and then fractures into a thousand tiny splinters that lodge into every atom of my body.

Fuck.

She doesn't say anything and neither do I.

Her colleague is probably in the bedroom.

All I can do is watch her as she goes about resetting the bar, scooping up my whisky glass from last night—the drink I used to take the edge off the frustration of being at her apartment and not being able to do what I wanted to her, with her, together.

When she's finished at the bar, she starts to wipe down other surfaces, cleaning them free of dust. She starts at the bar and works her way around the room in sections from top to bottom.

I'm mesmerized by the movement of her hem as she bends and stretches. At one point she keeps her legs quite straight and picks something off the floor; her skirt rides up so high, I can almost see her panties. Is she deliberately teasing me?

I shift in my chair. I can't take my eyes off her. She ignores me completely. Doesn't glance over at me once. She moves along the room counterclockwise, dusting as she goes, lifting up magazines and lamps, bending to catch the bottom of floor lamps and the legs of chairs and side tables.

She works thoroughly and consistently, and she's graceful and sexy and I can't stop looking at her.

She edges ever closer to me, but I don't move. She must know I'm watching her. She must feel my eyes on her.

She crouches beside my chair and dips underneath, her ass on perfect display, right next to me. If I reached out, I could grab—

Before I can form a thought, she maneuvers herself closer and brushes my thigh with her hand.

"Sorry, sir. I want to make sure I don't miss a spot."

It takes everything I have not to groan and pull her ass into my lap.

But I still don't know if we're alone. Surely she wouldn't risk us being seen?

She leans across me to get to my desk, her heavy breasts dangerously close to my mouth.

"Efa..." I rumble.

"I just need to get a little"—she steps between my thighs and reaches up behind me—"closer." Her skirt rides up higher and higher, and if I dip my head, just a little, I can see black lace.

She turns, still between my thighs, and leans over the desk.

My self-control tunnels into oblivion.

I slide my hand up her inner thigh and she continues to arrange my desk. Let's see how long she can pretend I'm not touching her.

"Are we alone?" I scratch out.

She nods but doesn't say anything. I trust her. I trust that she wouldn't put either of us in a situation where anyone could discover us like this. Maybe she hasn't earned that trust. I don't know her well enough, but my gut tells me she gets it. She's not going to expose us in any sense of the word.

My fingertips slip from her soft skin to the delicate lace of her underwear. She pauses for just a second before picking up the telephone receiver and wiping her duster over it.

I slide my fingers over her folds, finding her hot and wet and perfectly ready for my dick.

"You want it so bad," I say.

"You're right, sir," she says in a singsong voice. "I'm desperate to have everything dust-free for you."

My breaths are heavy and needy. She sways her hips, pushing my fingers deeper. I reach my arm around her thigh and find her clit.

"I think it's my dick you want."

She whimpers.

"I think you can't get enough. I think you're so fucking desperate to get fucked you'd do anything."

"By you," she blurts, circling her hips.

"What?" I snap.

"I'm desperate to get fucked by you. Only you."

I push my chair away and stand. If that's what she wants, that's what she's going to get. I've tried to resist this woman. I've tried to do the right thing. She knows in no uncertain terms that I'm not going to put her on the Fort payroll, yet still here we are, my fingers covered in her.

I grab my wallet from the desk and clumsily fumble for a condom. There's not time for me to feast on her. We both need release.

I need to fuck.

She needs to be fucked.

We both need to come or... god only knows what's going to happen.

I yank down her panties and push up the skirt of her dress so it bunches around her waist. In an effort to try to prove that I'm still in control, I press the crown of my condom-covered cock down through her soaking folds, once, then twice, before I push into her.

"Jesus Christ," she calls out.

"Be quiet," I grunt.

Bells ring in my ears. I tighten my jaw and grip her hips. I feel like I'm about to unravel. Like she's a kitten and I'm a ball of yarn and she's got the end of me between her teeth.

She's stripped me of my self-control, had me walk back on the promise I made to myself that I'd never be tempted to use my position of power or wealth to take advantage of anyone or anything. Even though she's assured me she wants this—wants me to fuck her, not because I'm Ben Fort, or because she thinks it will help her land her dream job—it's not good enough. Growing up in Hollywood, I saw men use and abuse their power. I swore I'd never do it.

Then along came Efa.

She feels so perfect, so tight. Her sounds echo around me, piercing through the ringing in my ears. She reaches one hand back, pressing her hand over mine, like she's feeling something more, something deeper—a connection.

I curl my hand into hers and thrust into her over and over. She whimpers, gripping my hand, my cock, and my chest from the inside out.

Fuck... this girl.

"No more teasing," I say. "This is what you wanted. This is what you practically begged for."

She's panting, so close to the edge that I know she'll be undone in seconds.

And thank god, because I can't hold it together any

longer. I need to be pressed up deep inside her, ripping her orgasm from her so I can have mine.

She trembles beneath me, her legs begin to shake. "Oh god," she cries out. "Oh god," she cries again, panic in her voice. It's like she's turning to liquid in my hands, I thrust up, up, up and follow her over the edge, my orgasm crashing over me like a landslide.

Shit.

We stay, bent over the desk, panting until our breaths even out.

I shift, already craving her tight heat as I slide out of her. She stands and smooths down her skirt. She turns, her face flushed, her legs still damp with a mixture of me and her. I can't take my eyes off her.

The condom in my hand, I continue to stare. She looks up at me from under her lashes, like she's back to being the submissive maid.

My jaw clenches. "Show me your pussy," I growl.

Her eyes narrow in confusion, but she gathers her skirt up her thighs to reveal her underwear.

I nod in appreciation. Already I want her again. Once wasn't enough. I'm staring at her panties. "Let me see."

I groan as I see how her wetness has darkened the lace, and then she pulls the fabric free of her pussy so I get to see the bare flesh I'm already craving again. My heartbeat is rattling in my chest. If I can't have her again, she's going to feel me all day as she works.

I upend the condom and my come drips out onto the lace; bright white evidence of what just happened between us.

She gasps and looks up at me, then bites down on her lip. I lift my chin slightly in victory and she blinks, long and slow, like she's dizzy with desire.

I drop the condom into the trash and she lets go of her panties with a snap. She'll feel my come on her pussy every step she takes for the rest of the day. The thought makes me want to beat my chest, lock the door, and do nothing but fuck her again and again and again.

I zip up my pants and buckle my belt.

She tilts her head slightly and smooths down her skirt. "Is there anything else I can do for you... sir?"

All I can do is growl at her, and just as I'm about to suggest she gets on her knees, the whir of the suite door's lock pulls our attention, and we both snap our heads around. I feel like a naughty schoolboy who's about to get caught with his hand in the candy jar, but I wouldn't take any of it back.

She picks up her duster from where she's dropped it on the floor and scurries over to the couch. I flip open my laptop.

The blood in my ears is pounding, my orgasm still whispering in the distance as I stare at the screen.

This is my fucking hotel, and I don't care what anyone thinks of me, but I don't want to get Efa into trouble. I imagine bending over for guests is frowned upon.

The older woman comes through the door and heads to Efa. Is she going to suspect? I can't imagine anyone can fuck like that and not have the aftermath showing somewhere—a graze on her neck, a rumpled uniform, the scent of lust.

But I only hear the two of them moving around the suite. After just a couple of minutes, they disappear, and I can breathe again.

TEN

Efa

Every time I come into the corridor from the Avenue Suite to go to my trolly, I can't help glancing at the Park Suite. It still doesn't have the light on requesting the room to be serviced like it has for the previous two days.

Is he not in there?

Is he trying to avoid seeing me?

I know it's pathetic, but I'm disappointed. Yesterday, his hands on me, his mouth by my ear, whispering such dirty things, his hips pinning me down—his come in my underwear.

It was...

He is...

I know I've slept with the guy on two separate occasions and I barely know anything about him, but there's something in me that needs more. If I'd had a one-night stand before, maybe I could compare. I'd know that it's normal to be left yearning, normal to want to *know* the man who just made you come.

I slip my hand into the pocket of my uniform dress and finger the printed copy of my résumé that I've been considering leaving with Bennett. As a recent graduate with zero experience, I know I don't have much to offer. But a job with Fort Inc. would fulfill a long-held dream. Surely I have to shoot my shot?

I'd be lying if I said I hadn't expected him to drop by the flat last night. Maybe a quick fuck over his desk is all he wanted, but I was a minute away from handing Gretal my resignation and locking the door for the day after what happened. I wanted to spend the rest of the week, the rest of the year, naked with Bennett.

Maybe he didn't feel the same. How could he not? Maybe sex with older men is always... electric, but I've never experienced anything like it. We were so in sync. He knew what I needed without me having to say anything. He knows just how hard to bite, how much to push, when to tease and when to just fuck the living daylights out of me.

Maybe it's American men. When people ask me what my type is now, I'm going to say rich, older Americans who fuck me like Bennett Fordham. Or Ben Fort, depending who he is in my head that day.

"Is that light on?" Marcella calls from inside the Avenue Suite.

"Let me check," I reply, pulling out a spare loo roll.

Of course I don't need to check. I know it's not on. And it's late.

"Not yet," I say as I head back into the bathroom and pull off the almost-finished roll of loo paper from the holder and replace it with the one I'm holding.

"I guess he has a meeting or something," she says.

"Or something."

I get a gnawing sensation in my gut and I can't decide if

it's because I feel bad there's a chance Bennett might be ignoring me, or because I haven't seen him today.

"I don't know what's wrong with this thing," Marcella says, shaking the tablet that tells us which rooms are occupied and which have checked out. I'm ninety percent certain that turning it into a techno snow globe isn't going to help, but you never know. Tech is fickle.

"What's happening?" I ask.

"Every time I try and update the rooms, it crashes."

Her phone bleeps, and she answers while I take the tablet and switch it off. It's a cliché, but sometimes hardware needs a timeout so it can come back in a better mood.

Marcella listens. "Totally crashed, yeah. Oh wow. Oh okay. Yes, yes." She glances at me. "Yes of course, I'll tell her." Then she ends the call. "Systems are down," she says. "It's not just room updates. The reservations system is totally screwed."

"That's weird," I say. I suppose it makes sense that there's an interface between the booking and room-update systems. I don't know why I do it—just a niggle of suspicion —but I pull out my phone and bring up the hotel website.

It's down.

Now, *that* doesn't make sense. There's no way an informational website would be linked with the booking system and the room-update system.

"Yeah, so reception doesn't know who's supposed to be checking in or out, and how many rooms there are to sell. They need extra hands on reception. Apparently, you're supposed to head down there ASAP."

"Oh," I say, glancing at the door of the Park Suite. I'm really not going to see Bennett today. "Are you going to be okay doing all this on your own?"

"Sure," she says.

"Shall I finish up here with you?" I ask. I should have put my résumé in an envelope. Then I could have slipped it under his door.

But maybe fate is my friend here. I'm not going to have a chance to give him my résumé. And maybe that way I'll save face. He probably would have laughed looking at my measly, one-page CV. No doubt he gets thousands of them, all more impressive than mine.

"Just go now or I'll get into trouble. But thanks," Marcella says. "You've been great."

I do my best to smile. "Thanks for all the help. You're the best, Marcella."

I turn and head out of the service door, giving the Park Suite one final look.

When I get to reception, I'm handed a plastic-wrapped uniform and directed to the basement to change. As I tear open the package, I wonder if Bennett ever has any need to come to reception. Probably not. Although, other than check people in and out, I have no clue what reception does.

There are two other women in the changing room and they look like they have the same uniform as me. I haven't been paying attention to the different uniforms throughout the hotel. Housekeeping feels a little removed from the rest of the staff, even though we're right in the heart of it.

"I can't freaking believe I'm here," the girl with the high pony says. "I should never have answered my phone."

"Why didn't you just make up an excuse?" says the woman with short brown hair. "I would have told them I was out of state or something."

"Yeah, I wasn't thinking straight," High Pony admits. "The entire reason I took this job was because Jessie has never been called in on a day off."

"I've never heard of a booking system going down,"

Short Hair says. "Not in a hotel of this size. Did you ever have it happen at the Mandarin?"

She shakes her head. "They better get it back up quick, because it's going to be a shit show out there."

She's right. I don't even know how you check people in if you don't have a booking system. High Pony looks in my direction as I tuck in my blouse.

"You working reception too?" she asks.

I nod. "Coming from housekeeping, so it's going to be a baptism of fire. Does it happen a lot? The booking system going down?"

The woman with short hair laughs and High Pony says, "If it did, I wouldn't be working here. We're going to take a lot of shit for this when it's not even our fault. It's impossible to run a hotel and not have a good booking system."

Short Hair snarks, "So maybe we're not working in a good hotel?" They share a little smirk before heading to the door.

I wish I could help beyond being just another pair of hands on reception. If only Gretal knew she had one of the most successful men in tech checked into the Park Suite. I bet Fort Inc. could have the system back up in a nanosecond.

ELEVEN

Bennett

Leo's apartment looks like the apartment a teenage boy would imagine in his head, apart from the fact that there aren't pictures of half-naked women on the walls. Well, there are, but they're black-and-white photographs in expensive frames, not dogeared posters. There's the biggest TV screen I've ever seen on one wall, and right next to it is a smaller screen—presumably so he can game and watch TV simultaneously? A bar at the other end of the room is only a little smaller than the one at my hotel—the one where I met Efa.

I was on calls all morning and couldn't request housekeeping until later in the day. Efa wasn't with the older woman when she finally arrived. It took me by surprise how disappointed I was. I even picked up my phone to message her and ask her where she was, but I realized I didn't have her number.

Where did she go?

"Beer?" Leo asks, stepping behind the gigantic bar.

"Am I the first here?" I sit down on the black velvet couch and spare half a thought for what residual substances I'm currently coming into contact with. I bet this couch has seen things no one should. To say Leo is a player is like saying Satan isn't the kind of man you want to bring home to Mom.

"Of course you're the first one here. This is our thing. We have a few minutes before the rest of the pack arrives."

I nod. He's right. It's often the two of us together early. And today it's not entirely by accident.

"How's your love life?" I ask him, taking the beer he offers and glancing around the place.

He chuckles. "Absolutely dandy, thanks."

"Do you ever sleep with anyone more than once?" I ask.

"Sure," he says. "Generally I have a regular-Tuesday-evening thing with someone. A sometimes-Friday thing with another. And then they cycle in and out. You know."

I don't. But I don't say anything.

"I picked up this girl the other night and called her to come over last night. That's not usually my thing. But she's fucking hot."

I half zone out of Leo talking about women. It's not why I asked the question.

"How young is too young for you?" I ask.

He laughs. "Why do I get the feeling you're trying to feel better about yourself by comparing yourself to me?" He doesn't sound offended. That's the thing with Leo—he knows who he is and he's totally fine with it.

"If that's what I'm doing, I'm an asshole. But I don't think I am. I think I'm just trying to..." There are so many reasons why lusting after Efa is wrong. The age thing is the biggest.

Before I can finish my sentence, Worth appears. Leo

leaves his door unlocked most of the time. I hope he's more careful about condoms than he is about home security.

"What's going on?"

"Bennett's fucking a younger woman and wants to feel better about it," Leo says.

Worth raises his eyebrows. "How young?"

"How young is too young?" Leo asks. "That's the question. What do you think, Worth?"

"We're not talking underage, are we?" Worth asks.

I choke on the mouthful of beer. "No!" I half yelp, half gasp.

Worth nods and bends to take a bottle of wine from the wine fridge—a fraction of Leo's wine collection, the rest of which is stored off-site. "That's good. Because that would be..." He shivers. "Out of character and just gross."

"I agree," I say. "But very early twenties?"

"Nice," Leo says.

"Don't be a dick about this," I say, my tone even. Because I'm actually serious. I want their opinion and we all have this bantery, jokey relationship, but we're also there for each other when shit gets real. And I want to discuss this.

Leo sighs like he's giving up on trying to make jokes. "You're thirty-four. Early twenties is no big deal. It's ten years."

Worth joins us on the sofa with an empty glass, a corkscrew and the bottle of wine—an Argentinian malbec. It's a favorite of mine and I sent it to all of them at Christmas.

"Twelve to be exact."

"Because you did a background check on her," Leo says.

Of course I did a background check. It's what I do. It's who I am. "But in your early twenties... you're... still figuring stuff out." What do I care if Efa is figuring stuff out? It's not like I'm considering dating her. I'm not going to ask her to dinner. Marry her. I just want to maybe, possibly, see her naked again. So why am I so intent on discussing this?

"Do we ever age out of figuring stuff out?" Worth asks, and it catches me by surprise. Worth is one of the most together people I know. Maybe that says more about the people I know than Worth. "We're human beings. The bar is always being raised. Ten years can be an ocean or it can be a puddle." He shrugs, scoots forward on the sofa, and sets to work opening the wine.

"A puddle?" I ask.

"Yeah, it depends on who you are and life experience. If you dated a woman who was twenty-one, lived at home with her parents in rural Alabama where she was home-schooled, it's going to be different to you dating a woman who has more in common with you. Someone who's done some living, even at a relatively young age."

"Right," I say.

"Are you dating her?" Worth asks.

I shake my head.

"Interesting," Leo says.

"Why is it interesting?" I ask.

"I've known you a long time. You've never talked about a woman you were actually dating. And here we are, talking about a woman you *want* to date."

"I didn't say I wanted to date her."

Both Leo and Worth chuckle.

"What? I've slept with her. And... I don't know. I wanted to know if I shouldn't have because, you know, her age and..."

"And... what?"

"And she wants a job."

Leo slides his beer bottle onto the table. "A job where?"

"At Fort Inc.?"

Worth slides his drink next to Leo's like they both need to have their hands free for what's about to happen.

"She knows you work at Fort?" Leo asks.

I pull in a breath and nod. This is such a can of worms. I'm not sure I should have opened it.

"Fuck," Worth says.

Leo and I both turn to look at Worth, who looks right at me.

"She knows you're Ben Fort," he says.

Leo gasps like he's just seen a dead body.

"I didn't tell her," I say. "She figured it out."

Leo's eyebrows crawl up to his hairline and his eyeballs look like they're about to pop out of his fucking skull. "She figured it out? How the fuck did a twenty-one-year-old figure it out when the world media hasn't been able to?"

It's a good question.

"She didn't know when I fucked her. The first time."

"And then she figured it out and you fucked her again?" Leo asks. "I'm surprised you didn't have her arrested and deported to the middle of the Atlantic Ocean. So, what, she knows and it's no big deal? Did you get her to sign an NDA?"

I let out a hollow laugh. "Actually no."

"What?" Worth asks, standing up like someone just put a cattle prod up his ass.

"She pointed out that an NDA isn't going to stop her talking if that's what she wants to do."

"It's stopped all your employees talking."

"Maybe," I reply.

"Maybe?" Leo asks.

"I think they keep quiet partly out of the legal obligation, but when I spoke to Efa, she made me see that an NDA can't actually do much. I think my employees don't talk out of loyalty. Any of them could have made a lot of money by telling people who I am."

"And... *Efa* made you see this?" Leo asks.

I grin. "Yeah, I guess she did... when she mocked me for asking her to sign the NDA."

"I like this girl," Leo says. "Sounds like she knows how to run rings around you."

Was that her appeal? Is that why I was sitting here chatting to my best friends about her when I'd never discussed any woman with them before? Because she showed me how flimsy the NDA was? Because she had an ass that hypnotized me? Or because she figured out who I was? "I guess," I reply. "I don't know her that well."

But not because she hides anything.

"Sounds like she knows you *very* well."

Maybe that's it. Maybe the fact that she figured out who I am makes me wonder what else she sees. In me. In others. In the world.

"I don't know if the NDA is worth pursuing," I say. "I don't even know what pursuing means. I don't think she's in the country long, and anyway, if she's not working for Fort, she's going to be working with a rival or a customer. That brings with it a whole heap of problems."

"Yeah, just give up," Worth says. It's such an un-Worth thing to say, I can tell he's mocking me. "Sounds like you. A quitter."

"I'm just saying. It's complicated."

"Life's complicated," Worth replies.

"Mine isn't," Leo says.

"If it isn't, it will be," Worth says.

"I'm not saying I want to marry this girl," I say.

Worth frowns. "Woman."

I nod. Worth's right. "So if we're not worried about the age difference, what about the power differential? She wants a job at Fort. I don't want to be fucking someone because they want a job from me."

"I'm not sure I'm the one to help you here," Leo says. "I've never analyzed any of my relationships that closely."

Worth's eyes slice to mine, but neither of us says anything. Leo has had a complicated life, but he chooses simplicity these days.

"I think you should trust your gut," Worth says. "If you thought she was assuming her skills in the bedroom would get her a job, you wouldn't be sleeping with her."

"Right," I say. I'm pretty sure the sex we had the first time is the reason Efa wanted to have sex again. My skin starts to buzz just thinking about her bent over my desk, uniform pushed up over her ass.

I clear my throat before I start getting a boner in front of these guys, which is just gross.

But whatever's between me and Efa isn't just sex. If it was, I'm pretty sure I could figure it out on my own. I wouldn't have brought it up here. Efa has complicated my brain. Why am I still thinking about her? Why am I so keen to delve beneath the surface? Why was I so disappointed when I didn't see her today?

"I think your gut will know better, the more you get to know her," Worth says.

"You're right. So are we going to watch sports or what?" I ask, just as the door goes again and Fisher and Byron appear. I'm done discussing this. I've made my decision. When everyone's settled, I'll head out. Go and see her—take the NDA. Just one more time, maybe my gut will be able to tell for certain why I can't get this woman out of my mind.

TWELVE

Efa

I smooth down my new black pencil skirt—that I only just fit into—and widen the fake smile I've been wearing all afternoon. I've learned I prefer housekeeping to reception. For more reasons than one.

"Enjoy your stay," I say, handing the woman in front of me a room key. At least rooms are still locking. It's pretty much the only thing that's working in this place.

Being moved to reception is so annoying. First, it means I finally got on top of my jet lag and now they've moved my shifts to the evening, which means I'm starting work when London is having cocktails. On top of that, every guest I deal with is pissed off because we can't find anyone's booking. We basically have to do a search on email confirmations to work out where everyone belongs, and it takes forever. Apparently there's a team hard at work piecing it all together on paper, which should be ready tomorrow, but shouldn't they really be focused on getting the booking system up and running? I don't know much about Gretal, but she needs to do something.

I hate people. I hate late nights. I especially hate that I haven't seen Bennett for two days. And I hate that I hate I haven't seen him.

I go round and round in my head about why I'm so disappointed that I've not laid eyes on him for just a few days. Is it the sex? That's got to be part of it. It's like the man invented my body, so he knows his way around it with his eyes closed. It's probably something to do with the fact that I haven't had the opportunity to give him my résumé. It's both those things, but it's something else too. Something I haven't quite figured out.

"Good evening, sir, are you checking in?" I ask the elderly man who comes up to the desk.

"No," he snaps. "Just tell me how to get to the bar."

"The hotel bar?" I clarify.

"Of course the hotel bar, you silly girl."

I pull in a breath, trying to calm myself, when I hear a familiar growl. I look up and my heart inches higher in my chest as I lock eyes with Bennett.

Bennett.

Bennett.

My entire body softens slightly in his presence. I no longer care about the rude man in front of me or the fact that I'm having to keep my eyes open by digging my nails into my palm.

"The sign for the bar is just there, sir," Bennett says. "Why don't I take you?"

Bennett doesn't strike me as someone who helps old men down to bars, but maybe I'm wrong. Maybe he's not swooping in like a knight in shining armor, saving me from a rude guest. But it sure feels like that.

I can't help hoping I'm right.

Still, I'm disappointed that I only caught a glimpse of him. And as I'm on reception, that's probably all I'll catch of him from now on. Until he checks out.

A woman in her thirties who I've seen before comes over to the desk. "I've lost my room key. Can I get a new one?"

"Certainly. Let me just ask you some security questions." When I'm able to bring up her email confirmation, I go through the questions about her stay, trying to surreptitiously glance toward the lobby to see if Bennett has come back up from the bar. Maybe he headed out.

To dinner perhaps? With his wife? Or girlfriend?

I really don't know anything about him. Apart from the fact he's a billionaire and owns one of the greatest minds ever known. Oh, and that he's Ben Fort. No big deal.

I hand the woman in front of me a new room key and she heads off.

I struggle to pull my glance from the corridor, checking for Bennett, as the next person approaches my desk.

Finally, I smile and look up—and realize I'm looking right at Bennett. By his expression, he totally knows what I was doing.

"Hi," I say, trying not to laugh at being completely caught out.

"Looking for someone?" he asks.

I smile up at him, and for the first time today, the expression is completely genuine. "Absolutely not," I say. "Not now. How may I help you this evening, sir?"

He pulls in a breath and his chest seems to grow bigger. "I want to book a table at a restaurant."

My stomach dips slightly and I'm not sure why. "My colleagues on the concierge desk can help you with that."

"But is there anywhere specific you recommend?" he asks, ignoring my implied suggestion that I can't help him.

My smile falters a little. I don't know how to read him. What is he asking me? "Sir, I'm new to New York. I've not had much experience dining in the city. But my colleagues would be happy to help you."

He nods. "I'm sure. And when you're in London, what's your favorite restaurant?"

I'm still flummoxed. Is he such an awkward billionaire that he doesn't know how normal conversation works? "I'm not fussy. Rules is..." Rules was where our parents used to take us for our birthdays. It's comical really, because it's such a weird restaurant to take a kid to. All the waiters wear morning coats like they're in church for a wedding, and it's so old-fashioned. But I have happy memories from there— some of my only memories of my parents, actually, from when I was really young.

"Rules," he repeats.

"Yeah, it's a—"

"I know it," he says.

I cock my head. "You do? Do you spend a lot of time in London?" Somehow the idea of Bennett in London makes my stomach flip. He's so... American. I can't imagine him there.

"Of course," he says. "But that choice has thrown me a little. You like it there, huh?"

"Honestly, I'm not the best person to ask about restaurants on either side of the pond," I say. "Geoff on concierge seems to know every restaurant in New York."

Is Bennett... not familiar with the city? Even though Fort Inc.'s offices are right in Manhattan? Does he never eat out? Surely he must know where's good.

He holds my gaze, and I know I should look away but I

can't. I miss the moments of private time we had when I was cleaning his suite.

Oh, and the sex, and his come in my underwear.

"You're here now," he says.

At reception? In New York? I can't keep up with this man.

"I am," I say, and he winces, like that wasn't the right response. I'm frustrated. I want us to be able to speak openly. Freely. I want to be alone with him when I'm not in a uniform and he's not a guest.

"I hear Tribeca Grill is nice," I say, worried that if I don't say something, he'll have to leave and then what? I'll probably never see him again.

"Okay, good."

"Anything else I can help you with?" *Happy to come to your suite later and get naked and dirty*, I singsong in my head.

"Maybe later," he says cryptically.

Then he catches what my co-worker Jason is saying to a guest about the booking system.

"What's going on?" he asks, voice lowered.

"Systems are down. Booking system, room system. You name it."

"Hmm." His eyebrows pinch together. "The room system and the booking system. You'd think they'd be separate but talk to each other. Why would both go down at once?" He's half talking to himself, but it's exactly the question I asked myself.

"But more surprising is the fact that the hotel website is offline," I say. "That can't be a coincidence. And it's been off for a couple of days now." I shrug. "Maybe I'm paranoid, but it feels like... sabotage. Or something."

His eyes flare with anger. I've never seen his expression

so fierce. "You've been very helpful," he says, and he turns and leaves.

I can't believe that Bennett Fordham, a.k.a. Ben Fort, would get so angry about a website failure. What is the matter with him? At the end of my shift, maybe I can dress up as room service and go and knock on his suite door to find out what's really going on.

Or maybe I just have to resign myself to the fact that Bennett and I had sex a couple of times, and that was that.

THIRTEEN

Bennett

Seeing Efa at reception today was all the confirmation I needed that Worth and Leo were right. I need to know more about her. I don't know why I want to spend time with her. And I won't until I do more research. Undertake further investigations.

Which explains why I'm loitering in corridors at midnight.

I pull up my phone and check that the hotel website is back up and running.

If only I'd known the hotel's systems and site were down sooner, I could have done something about it. It would never happen at Fort Inc. If it's important, I know about it at Fort. But Fort Industries? It's more of an investment portfolio than a business. Samantha, one of my most trusted employees, oversees everything under that umbrella. The hotel, a couple of other businesses I've bought, the small investments I make into projects that help the environment or create communities.

I'm sure Samantha's aware of the issues at the hotel, but she hasn't told me about them. I respect her for wanting to sort them out herself, but I'm pissed that she let this shit show go for two days without reaching out. I solved the issue in a nanosecond. She can't know I did, otherwise she might put two and two together and figure out I have more contact with the hotel than I tell her. She obviously doesn't know I'm staying there.

So much secrecy. All necessary to protect the most important thing to me—my privacy.

How ironic that one of the few people who know who I am was the person to tell me about the problem.

I straighten.

Was it ironic? Or is it possible that Efa was the one who sabotaged the systems? Because sabotage is definitely what happened. There wasn't an error or a technical fault. Someone had deliberately brought the systems down. Without any ransom request.

While I'm here, I can have a further dig around. Part of furthering my investigations.

To see if it's her trying to fuck with me.

She rounds the corner from the elevator and her smile blooms on her face, and I feel it in my veins. If I listen to my gut, as Worth advised, there is nothing remotely suspicious about Efa. She's all sunshine and truth and honesty. I'm the liar in our relationship. But I have to go by the data, not my gut, and the coincidences are piling up.

"Hey," I say.

"It's nice to see you," she says and my head spins like I'm being tossed upside down on a carnival ride. I realize just how badly I wanted her to *want* to see me. "I've mis— It's been weird not seeing you in your suite."

She almost let it slip that she missed me. I bite back a smile. We're both hiding things.

She pulls out her keys and I step aside, letting her unlock the door. When she gets it open, she pauses, turns to curl her fingers around my wrist, and pulls me inside as if to make sure I'm not going anywhere.

"How was your day?" I ask.

She slips off her black stilettos and I kind of wish she hadn't. I mentally chastise myself. I shouldn't be thinking like that. I've got to get to the bottom of who she is and why she's popped up in my life *now*, of all times.

"Want a drink?" She heads to the kitchen area.

"Questionable red?" I ask.

"If I'd known you were coming, I would have got something better in. My brother-in-law owns a vineyard and he'd be horrified I'm not better stocked."

"Another brother-in-law?" I ask. "Is that code for something I don't understand? Or does it mean something different in the UK?"

She laughs as she fills two glasses of water from the faucet, no ice, then slides one across the counter toward me.

"My sister is almost married to a guy with five brothers. So I call all six of them brothers-in-law. Is that wrong? I keep meaning to look it up."

"And one of them owns a vineyard?"

"Yeah, in Argentina I think."

"Okay," I say cautiously, not knowing what to do with that information. Do I have to do anything? Is this "getting to know her"? I can't remember ever doing this with a woman. Chatting. About nothing. Without an aim or an expectation.

"So, you know how you told me about the hotel systems?" I ask.

Her face lights up—not because she's excited, just because she's engaged. "Yes. Isn't that weird? And the fact that the website was offline too. They should have been able to get that back up and running in like, a nanosecond." She shakes her head.

"What's that look for?" I ask. I really want to know what she's thinking, but I don't want to influence her by making a suggestion.

"It just feels—well, I guess I'm getting as paranoid as you. It's probably nothing. Everything is up again now anyway."

"No, something was bothering you. What is it?" I ask, trying to sound only vaguely interested. She specifically mentioned sabotage before, but why?

"The systems at the hotel are all back up and working again. Thank god."

"You said you were getting paranoid. Why?"

"It's just that a malfunction like this feels... deliberate. I mean, why a hotel website? It's not like it's a ton of complex code. The hotel isn't even a chain. I had a look at the website before I came out to New York—really simple stuff. That's not going to go down unless someone hasn't done their job in terms of maintenance. But if a maintenance issue caused the site to go down, it's easy to get it back up."

She's totally right.

"And why a hotel booking *and* room management system? Two systems that work together but are wholly separate. It feels deliberate. It has to be corporate ransom or something."

"Ahhh. You think it's ransomware."

"For sure," she says. "Don't you? I had a quick check online. There are no major issues out there. And then before I left tonight, the entire system came back up. Like someone paid their bill—or their insurance—and suddenly everything's working again."

She's not behind this. I can feel it in my bones. There's no way.

A feeling of relief settles over me and I feel my jaw unlock. I'm really fucking happy this isn't her doing.

"Except you normally hear about a ransom," I say. "The person holding you to ransom has to ask for money. Otherwise, what's the point?"

"Right. The owners of the hotel were probably contacted. And they paid."

"Except he wasn't and he didn't."

She narrows her eyes. "You own the hotel?"

I shrug. "One of my companies does."

She takes her glass and pads over to the sectional. "Wow."

"I wanted to be completely honest with you." I follow her and sit down as far away as possible. I don't trust myself not to touch her if I'm too close.

"Says the man who pretends to be someone he's not."

"I don't pretend," I say. "I'm always the same man. My name just changes in certain scenarios."

"But why?" she asks. It's a question my closest friends still ask, even though they know the reason. "For security reasons? Like... you don't want to be kidnapped?"

"Well, *obviously* I don't want to be kidnapped, but that's not the reason. I just don't want the attention. I don't want to be famous. Or well-known. Or recognizable."

"Okay. But *why?*" she asks.

I don't know where to start.

"You were so suspicious of me," she continues, "but I'm an open book. I should be suspicious of *you*. You're the one with all the secrets."

"Let's agree that ends now." I don't know what I'm saying. What I'm doing. All I know is that being close to her feels better than anything I've felt. Maybe ever.

A look of disappointment washes over her. "What does?"

"The secrets," I explain. "We both agree to be completely honest. From now on."

"From now on," she says, confused. "Until when?"

It's a good question. Something I would ask... normally. But I'm not in normal territory. "I don't know," I answer honestly. "But now, and for as long as we know each other, let's always promise to be honest." It's the unspoken bond I have with my friends. We're all completely and utterly honest with each other—and I know I can't have any deep, fulfilling relationship without that. Growing up in Holly-wood, I witnessed the exact opposite all the time. It was trickery and special effects, rehearsed lines and prosthetics. It didn't matter if it was on camera or not, the relationships were scripted. Fake. I want no part in that.

"If you say so. Doesn't really change anything for me."

I bite back a smile. "Yeah, you don't have much of a filter, do you?" So why did I feel it was necessary to have this honesty pact? Do I need her to know that *I'm* being honest now? Do I want her to trust me?

"I don't. But you still haven't answered my question about why you have two names. I'm guessing it's not the reason I have two names. You really should have chosen a better pseudonym. Ben Fort and Bennett Fordham are way too similar. Like, almost—do you *want* to be found out?"

I chuckle. "They are similar. When I first changed my name, I was young. I didn't expect Fort Inc. to be quite as successful as it has been. I probably would have picked something else if I had."

She listens to me, her attention rapt, her eyes darting around my face like she doesn't want to miss anything. "And? Why did you feel the need to change your name when you were young? Did you commit a crime? Escape prison?"

"I was famous by association. I wanted to break that link."

She groans. "Stop talking in circles. Just spit it out. Famous by association? What does that even mean?"

"My mother was famous. She died when I was nineteen. I wanted to escape her world and live my own life rather than be forever associated with her."

"Huh. How did she die?"

That's never the reaction I get when I tell people my mother died. People tell me they're sorry, or they try to console me. They never ask how she died. At least not right away. Efa continues to break the mold.

"She had cancer."

She nods. "So you had a build-up. Warning?"

Again, not the reaction I expected. "Some. She died about three months after the initial diagnosis." She winces and slides her hand over mine.

Silence winds around us as I savor the feel of her skin against mine. It's more comforting that the normal words of condolence people usually offer.

"My parents died when I was sixteen," she says. "Helicopter crash."

I close my eyes in a long blink. "Fuck," I say. I should have had the entire background check sent to me rather than just the highlights. She just nods, and neither of us speaks. We both get it. No one can ever say anything that will make it better, so why try?

"You got no notice," I say, understanding her reactions a little better now.

"No," she sighs. "And honestly, they weren't doting parents. It's not like they left a big hole—"

"Efa," I interrupt. "They were your parents."

"Yes, they were, and it was weird not having them there. It's just that I'm not sure I missed them, exactly. Life moved on much the same as it had. It was only when I went off to university that things... shifted. My uncle stole our money and, you know, from a practical point of view, things changed because we were broke. My sister suffered the brunt of it. She always protected me."

"Jesus, Efa. That's... rough."

She shrugs. "It was difficult at times. But things have shifted again, and when I'm twenty-five, I get my inheritance. I'll be fine from a financial perspective. I have my sister. And Dylan, my brother. I'm lucky."

I sigh. Lucky. I guess she is. But it's a very mature perspective from someone who's just twenty-one. "I'd describe myself as lucky too."

"You're a self-made billionaire. *I'd* describe you as lucky, too, although I'll admit it's probably a little more than luck in your case." She laughs. "But what about your dad? Is he still alive?"

Did she just compliment me? Kinda sorta? I'll take it. "I have no idea. My mother never told me who he was."

"Oh wow. And do you have siblings? Do they know?"

I push my hand across my chest. "No and no." Sometimes I yearned for siblings when I was younger, but in the end, being alone made it easier to disappear.

"You're the youngest?" I ask.

"Yeah." She shakes her head. "Wait. You didn't tell me

who your mother was. You said she was famous. Would I know her?"

"Kathleen Fordham," I say.

She sits bolt upright. "Kathleen Fordham was your mother! She's... she was so beautiful. And I love that movie she did with the other guy, the one with the—" She pulls at her chin. "Douglas Harrison."

I nod. *"The Rose and The Thorn."*

"That's it! I love that movie. Wow. You must be so proud."

She shot that movie when I was about ten and complained about it every single day. She never went into any details, but reading about Hollywood back then, it's not hard to guess why a gorgeous woman in her prime might have had a difficult time on set.

"I am proud."

Efa stands and takes a seat closer to me. "You promised to be honest, but I can hear the echo of something when you tell me you're proud. It's such an empty statement. What are you thinking?" She reaches forward and sweeps her fingers across my forehead, like she's trying to read my thoughts.

"Just that she hated making the movie, and I hated seeing her so surrounded by people who wanted something from her. Some of them would have sold their soul for a moment with her. To get to hold her hand or sign an autograph."

"Wow," she says, as if I've said something that means something important. "So that's why you changed your name. Because you didn't want people to want something from you. You don't want to be a commodity. But then you became wildly successful on your own merits and you're on the run again."

"On the run?"

"Hiding out in hotels," she says. "Lurking in corridors."

"I wouldn't describe it as hiding. Or lurking."

"Wouldn't you?" She cocks her head.

"No. I mean, I normally have an apartment. I'm only staying in the hotel because... I think I might have a stalker. I think someone might have made the connection between me and Ben Fort."

"Right. And you don't want to be discovered. So you're hiding."

"But it's not a permanent thing. This situation is temporary."

"But you're permanently not on the internet. I mean, everyone in tech has heard of Ben Fort, but no one can put a face to that name."

"My five closest friends can. People I went to business school with."

"People you went to business school with have seen you and know you're Ben Fort? Did you have to pay them all off not to shop you to the media?"

I laugh at how she cuts right to the heart of everything. "I'd trust them with my life. And rightly so. Nothing's ever come out."

She leans her elbow on the back of the sofa and stares at me, watching me like I'm some kind of exhibition.

"What?" I ask her.

"Just admiring the view. It's pretty unforgettable."

For a split second, I think she's talking about the New York skyline, but when our eyes meet, I realize she's paying me another compliment.

She knows who I am. She wants something from me—a job. But I don't sense anything but genuine interest from her in this moment.

She frowns and the moment is broken. "Do they know the hotel owner is staying at the hotel?"

I shake my head. "Gretal knows Fort Industries own the hotel."

"Right," she says. "And you're Bennett Fordham, nothing to do with Ben Fort. So the website is back up. The booking systems too?"

I nod. "Yeah, I just wish Gretal or Samantha had told me about the problem. I could have sorted it sooner. In fact, if you hadn't told me, I still might not know."

"See? If you gave me a job, I would be an asset." The sentiment is heartfelt, but her smile is teasing.

I sigh. I'm not sure if I can resolve that issue between us. She's always going to want a job from me. And I'm always going to wonder if that's why she's sleeping with me. I let out a growl of frustration. "I'm not giving you a job," I say.

She presses out her lips in an exaggerated pout. "Maybe not yet."

"Not ever. I should go."

"Because I asked for a job?" she asks.

"Because I'm here because..." I promised her honestly. "Because I want to be here. But did you let me in because you want a job?"

She pulls back. "No," she says, locking eyes with me deliberately. "I'm not sleeping with you to get a job." She leans in and kisses me, and I feel it inside and out. "I'm sleeping with you because the sex is phenomenal, and I like spending time with you—enigmas and all."

Another compliment. Two, in fact. I reach for her and slide her towards me.

"Wait," she says. "What was that when you were asking about restaurants at reception? Are you trying to tell me you're married or have a girlfriend or something?"

I laugh. Is that how it looked? "Absolutely not."

"Then what was with all the questions? You know I'm not a New Yorker."

I'm such a huge idiot. "Honestly?"

"I demand nothing but," she says with a smile.

"I was... trying to figure out if there's somewhere I could take you to dinner."

Her face brightens and she grins at me. "You were?"

I shrug. "But Tribeca Grill? I'm trying to lie low. That's not the place to do it." Her smile dissolves, and I can feel her disappointment in my chest, low and heavy. "I'm sorry. I'll try and think of something."

"I know a place."

"A place?" I ask.

"A place where you can take me on a date. Because I can tell you're desperate to."

I chuckle. It's like she's set fire to any filter she might have been born with. "Where?"

She shakes her head. "No. I'm not telling."

I go to object, but she presses her fingers against her lips. "Nope. But I know you're trying to lie low. So nowhere fancy, I promise. Tomorrow lunch. Does that work?"

"Lunch?" I ask. The time of day should be the last thing I'm worried about, but I had a vision of us dressing up and me flying her to Paris or something, followed by a soak in a tub full of rose petals and a night exploring each other's bodies.

An alarm sounds on her phone, and she swipes it silent. "I have to make a call," she says.

"You have a job in a hotel and have a scheduled call?" I ask, only half-jokingly. Does she have a date?

"With my sister. So unless you wanna meet the fam,

you better get going. Unless you're going to fuck me. Then I might let you stay."

I'm not going to fuck her. Not tonight, anyway.

I get to my feet, and as she moves away, I grab her hand and pull her toward me. I plant a kiss on her head. "Tomorrow. If I don't happen to see you as I go through reception."

"I'll be looking for you."

I hope she will be.

FOURTEEN

Efa

Obviously I can't meet him at the hotel, even though I'm only a block away, so I've agreed to meet him at the Madison Square Park fountain. I'm wearing sunglasses despite the overcast skies, and I'm reading an old copy of *The New York Times* that I found behind reception. I'm like something out of a bad spy movie, just waiting for him to find me.

A particularly dark cloud passes overhead and I shiver.

"Efa," Bennett says and pulls my newspaper from my hands. "What are you doing?"

I grin up at him. He looks so good. I've never seen him in anything but office attire, and I one hundred percent appreciate it. But today? It's hard not to look at him the way he's dressed. His outfit is simple: Levi's and a white t-shirt. Wayfarers and a Yankees cap. He's like an advert for Americana, and he wears it like a champ. His body is more on show like this. Easier to reach. Easier to touch.

I stand. "Hey. You look handsome."

"Doing the crossword?" he asks, stuffing the paper into the bin.

"It was part of my disguise."

He raises his eyebrows. "I'm disappointed there's no wig."

"Oh I'm sure I can find one for later." Maybe whips and chains don't do it for him, but roleplay does? "For now, it's just a newspaper and lipstick."

"The red looks good on you," he says.

I wink at him. "I'm glad you think so."

Our gazes lock, and for a second too long, I wonder why we bothered coming out to eat. Why didn't I suggest takeout in bed?

I smooth my hands over his arms, lift up on tiptoes and plant a kiss on his cheek, leaving a great big red lipstick mark on his cheekbone.

"Thanks. That's inconspicuous."

I laugh on a roll of my eyes and grab his hand, leading him to our eatery, just a couple of steps away.

As we get to the entrance, I stretch out my hand in a *voila* movement.

"Shake Shack?" he asks, reading the sign.

"We have one of these in London. Burgers are delicious."

He shakes his head with a chuckle and I lead the way, finding us a table at the edge of the outdoor seating area. "What can I get you?" I ask. "My treat."

"This is where you want us to have our first date?" he asks, genuinely surprised.

"First of all, we can't sit at Tribeca Grill, can we? You have pretty strict requirements. And second, this isn't our first date, Romeo. We've had sex twice. We've hung out. We've had conversations, shared things, pledged our honesty to each other. It's not a conventional getting-to-know-you—not by British standards, anyway. I'm rolling with it because I figure you're worth it."

"Worth it?" he asks. There's a trace of suspicion in his voice. I recognize it from when he thought I was stalking him by working in his hotel room. But he has nothing to be suspicious about. Not with me.

"Yeah," I say. "In the spirit of full honestly, I like hanging out with you. In all ways."

"All ways?"

"Naked ways and not-naked ways."

He grins, even though I can tell he's trying not to. "And at Shake Shack."

"Right," I say. "I'm going to order you the biggest burger I can find and then I'm going to order two for me. Back in a sec."

I make my way to the counter and look over my shoulder. He's staring at my arse and I love that for him—I wore my best jeans in anticipation of a moment like this. I'm taking it as a win.

I get our food and drinks and bring the piled-high tray back to the table.

"And when do your friends arrive?" he asks.

"Oh no, sir, most of this food is for me. I've skipped meals all day because I knew we were coming here."

"It's noon. How many meals could you possibly have skipped?"

"Three, duh." I'm grinning at him and our eyes lock. Even though his mouth is only slightly tilted upwards, the sparkle in those eyes tells me he's happy. And I'm happy he's happy.

We unpack our burgers and swap condiments and napkins and finally dig into the food.

He swallows and I watch his Adam's apple bob. "This is really good," he says.

"That's the problem with you billionaires. You don't know how to enjoy the small stuff. I keep telling you."

"You billionaires? Are there a lot of us in your life?" He laughs, but I'm about to rain on his parade.

"Well, there's Dax, the man my sister is engaged to. And—"

"Your sister is engaged to a billionaire?" His expression is doubting.

"Dax Cove. Look him up."

He pulls out his phone and starts typing. "Bitcoin billionaires. Two a penny."

"Except his day job is medical research—like, saving lives and stuff. The way I see it, he deserves to be a billionaire."

"Okay, so he's a billionaire."

"And then there are all his brothers—they're wealthy. I'm not sure how wealthy, but Vincent has a plane. He owns the place where I'm staying. But you probably know that already, since I'm certain you and your paranoia have checked me out."

He shrugs. "I check out everyone in my life."

"I get it," I say. "It's difficult to trust people. I'd rather trust—albeit taking precautions—and get taken advantage of, than live less of a life because I *can't* trust anyone."

He doesn't move his gaze from mine as he takes another bite of his burger.

"Tell me why you're staying in the hotel and you don't go into the office," I ask.

His gaze flits over my shoulder and then across to scan the restaurant.

"Precautions," he says. But he's not looking at me. He's looking everywhere *but* at me.

Have I pissed him off? Perhaps I shouldn't have said anything. He seems to be getting more and more uptight the more we sit here.

"Precautions about what?"

"I told you. I think someone's been following me."

"Right, but there must always be people who want to find you-know-who's real identity. Why are you being so cautious now?"

"A few things." He leans a little farther forward. "Does something feel off to you? It's like the air has shifted or something."

I glance around the restaurant and there's... definitely something happening. Someone shouts in the distance and a murmur waves through the diners. Staff appears, moving tables around.

Maybe the paranoia is catching, but I swear I can hear the sound of camera shutters going off everywhere. "Bennett," I whisper. "Did you hear that?"

He pulls in a breath and pulls down his cap. "I think we should leave." He definitely heard it.

At that exact moment, there's a little more activity at the entrance to the outdoor seating area. Some beefy-looking guys come through the gate and start looking around before a group of six to eight people follow.

I start to laugh as I recognize one of the faces amongst the group.

Bennett is half out of his seat.

"Sit down," I whisper. "This is not about you. Seems like Tom Cruise likes Shake Shack just as much as me."

He frowns in confusion. "What?"

"That's what the fuss is all about." I nod toward the

party of guys on the other side of the restaurant. "Tom Cruise is in the building."

Bennett finally lets out a chuckle, then sighs and sinks back into his seat. "Ahhh. I can enjoy this burger after all. I was thinking I might have to abandon my food, and that's never a good feeling."

I laugh and slot my legs between his, wanting to get closer to him and his smile. "Maybe this wasn't such a good idea."

"The burgers are great," he says, taking another bite.

"But you're not comfortable. I didn't expect you to be so... We should have ordered room service. Except then I'll get fired, which is only a big deal because I don't want to let down—"

"One of your numerous brothers-in-law."

"Right." I grin at him.

"We should get away for the weekend," he says.

"Like a romantical mini-break?" I suggest, picturing some country castle in Scotland.

"Somewhere in the middle of nowhere. A log cabin maybe."

"Oh yes, I love a lack of flushing toilet. It's just so intimate."

He chuckles. "It's your turn to be tense on our date."

"True," I reply. "If you want to take me away to a place without a flushing toilet, I would be delighted. I think I might follow you anywhere." He raises his eyebrows, and I replay my own words back in my head. "As in, because I can't get enough of you, not because I'm stalking you. For the record. In case that required clarification."

He laughs again, and the sound washes over me like warm water and bubbles. "How can I resist a challenge like that?"

FIFTEEN

Efa

The build-up to this trip has been the best. The idea of being with Bennett for an extended period of time has me... fizzing inside. If I wasn't a little afraid of where we're going —and being forced to shit in the woods—I might actually be giddy.

I'm cross-legged in the passenger seat of a huge SUV, noticing fewer and fewer houses as we keep driving. We seem to have been going for hours.

"We must be nearly there by now," I say.

Bennett chuckles. "Not even a little bit."

I groan. "Why don't you just tell me where we're headed and then I can track how long it will take to get there?"

"You said you wanted to have some fun this summer. Not knowing where you're going to end up is part of the adventure."

I laugh out loud thinking of how Eira, my sister, would

react to that statement. Bennett would be put in the box marked *Serial Killer* for sure. "If you say so."

"Let me in on the joke," he says.

I grin at him, slightly delighted that he can read me so well.

"Just that if my sister was here, she'd assume you were driving me into the woods to murder me."

He nods. "Yeah, I get that. Haven't known you that long. Won't tell you where we're going. Secret identity. You haven't met any of my friends. It doesn't look good."

I narrow my eyes at him. "You have friends?" I say in mock shock. "Bennett Fordham, I don't believe you."

He laughs. "That's the part you focus on in all that? I hate to disappoint you, but it's true."

"I can't imagine you'd trust anyone enough to have actual friends." I reach over and place my palm on his forehead like I'm checking for a temperature. "Are you sure they're not hired help?"

"Oh I wouldn't want to hire them." He catches my hand as I lower it, twisting his fingers through mine. "Total bunch of reprobates. Known them since business school."

As he faces the windscreen, I take in the lines at the corners of his eyes, the twitch at the corner of his mouth. Happy Bennett is a sight to behold.

"But I trust them," he says. "With my life."

"It's nice you have that. I feel the same about my brother and sister. But I'm not sure about my friends."

"Really? I would have thought you have a thousand friends. I should be the one alone in my hermit cave."

"Nope. It's my name over the cave entrance. Not that I'm a hermit. Just that I can be a bit slow to let people in."

"Really?" he asks.

"Really. Somehow not with you. But usually. Since my

uncle stole our inheritance." I'd already told him the full story: After my parents died, their assets were put in trust for us to have when we each turned twenty-five. Everything had seemed okay until Eira's twenty-fifth birthday. She was expecting to inherit, and instead we found out our uncle was a crook and had taken everything.

"Yeah, that makes sense. I'm still confused about him leaving all the money to you when he died. How does that make sense?"

"When we were going through the house, we found a letter he'd written, apologizing. He wrote it when he knew he didn't have long to live. He said he'd never had any intention of taking the money, but he'd gotten addicted to the way people treated him differently when he was managing the estate. He said it wasn't the luxury lifestyle so much as how people looked at you when you had all the accoutrements of wealth."

"Accoutrements of wealth, huh?"

I beam at him. "Big-Word Efa, that's what they call me."

He chuckles. "I bet they do." He taps his fingers on the steering wheel. "It's interesting that he felt the shift and... got addicted to it. I think one of the reasons I have the friendship circle I do is that we all share similar attitudes toward wealth. None of us especially likes the special treatment... although Leo might be the exception."

He ends his sentence, but I can tell there's more. Something deeper. Something that's been there a long time. "I bet your mum was treated differently before and after she was famous."

"I imagine she was. I never knew her as anything but movie star Kathleen Fordham."

"She was a movie star, even to her son?"

"No, but she was successful from before I was born. She

didn't act like anything but a mother with me. And she was as present in my life as a working mother could be in her situation. I have no resentment there." He slides a hand over my thigh. Although we haven't spoken about it in detail, it's like he knows there's some resentment inside me for my parents—the lack of attention they paid any of us.

"My resentment was all directed at the people around her. From a really young age, I just knew these people didn't love my mother the way they pretended to. I saw through it. Maybe I picked up on how her relationships changed subtly and not so subtly, depending on her box office success. Or failure. She had her fair share of bombs back in the day."

"So you're careful about who you trust. That makes sense," I say. I can't help but wonder whether his reaction is still ruling his life, making it more difficult than it should be. "And here we are, driving hours out of the city so we can just... be."

"It's not always like this. Usually I can go about my day and no one knows who I am. But there have been a couple of break-ins at my apartment building, and it feels like someone's definitely watching. Waiting. Until I figure out who and why, I'm taking precautions."

I nod resolutely. "Precautions that involve a flushing toilet?" I ask.

He chuckles. "Maybe. Maybe not."

"Why are you being so secretive?" I ask. He won't tell me anything about where we're going except that it's in the country. What does that even mean? I'm betting the American version of the country is very different to the British version, which is full of sheep, stone cottages, and roads only wide enough for one car to pass along.

His eyes slice to mine and then he smiles. "I just want you to be surprised."

"I'm going to be surprised if we're sleeping under canvas and eating cold baked beans out of a can. And not in a good way."

He laughs out loud. "Why does it feel kinda good to torture you?"

"Because you're a serial killer in the making?"

He shakes his head but doesn't say anything. I want to ask him what he's thinking. I want to know whether he feels as comfortable with me as I do with him. I want to slip inside his brain and understand what exactly is going on in there.

"Is it a log cabin?" I ask.

He nods. "It is, actually."

"That's how I imagine America in the woods. At least we won't be under canvas." After a beat, I ask, "Will we sleep in a bed? Or on the floor?" I ask.

"Oh, I don't have any intention of sleeping very much at all." His hand rides high up my thigh, and I feel the heat spreading across my chest and up my neck.

"Sounds like my kind of log cabin."

SIXTEEN

Bennett

Lucky for me, I have friends like Worth, who I trust with my life. And even luckier for me, Worth has a taste for luxury, peace, and quiet. A perfect combination in my circumstances.

"This is some kind of log cabin," Efa says as we pull up to Worth's place. I've never been here before, but I knew it wasn't going to be a dump. "It's huge."

We get out of the car and take in our surroundings.

She turns around a full three hundred and sixty degrees, gazing up at the towering oaks and pretty maples that surround us. "And the perfect place to murder me." Her gaze catches on mine and she tilts her head, a softness in her eyes. "I love this kind of surprise."

I hold out my hand and she darts over to me, taking both my hands in both of hers.

We take the couple of steps up to the wraparound porch, which is smattered with Adirondacks, upended logs used as side tables, and a hammock. It's simple and looks rustic, but it's beautiful.

"Have you ever been here before?" she asks.

"Never," I say. I've never taken a woman away before. Before Efa, I would never have considered it. The thought of being with a woman in an isolated place wouldn't have sounded fun to me before.

I stand aside and let Efa go in before me.

"Wow," she says.

The inside of the structure is all wood and logs, but there's a modern kitchen, statement light fixtures, and loads and loads of space.

"This is gorgeous."

I knew it would be. It's Worth's place, after all. He's all about understated luxury. But I'm pleased Efa is so obviously thrilled.

"Let me check about the loo," she says, dashing off.

I grab the bags from the car and bring them inside. As I set them down, Efa comes running at me and jumps into my arms, wrapping her legs around me.

"Flushing toilets. You know how to spoil a girl."

I squeeze her ass, enjoying the feeling of contentment I get more and more when she's with me. "Worth also said there's a hot tub, a sauna, and an ice barrel."

She unlocks her legs from me and slides down to the ground. "You had me until ice barrel. You're on your own there. But happy to test out the hot tub and sauna with you. Sounds like there are plenty of places to get naked."

I growl at her words. "There won't be enough nakedness for me on this trip."

She lifts up on her toes and gives a quick press of her lips against mine. It's not enough. It's never enough from her.

Like she knows what I'm thinking, she laughs and picks up her bag. "I need to freshen up a little."

I take her bag from her and we go and check out the bedrooms, settling on a room that's large with a four-poster bed made out of logs, but is clearly not the master.

"Give me a minute, will you?" she asks.

I turn and go back to the kitchen. Worth has a house-keeping service, and I've arranged for a fully stocked refrigerator. We don't have to leave this place while we're here.

I open the fridge and try to figure out what we can have for lunch.

"This naked enough for you?" Efa says.

I turn to find her entirely nude, her hand on her hip, standing in the middle of the living room, her golden hair tumbling over her shoulders.

My breathing falters, and all I can see is her.

She beckons me forward with a curl of her finger. Like I'm in a trance, I step toward her.

"Looks like you've got far too many clothes on," she says. "Let me help you with that."

I tip my head back as she slips her fingers beneath my waistband and undoes the button on my jeans. She slides the denim over my hips, pulling my briefs down with them. She kneels before me, taking off my shoes, socks, and then my pants, so I'm naked from the waist down.

My cock rears in front of her, and I pull off my t-shirt in one swift movement. She remains kneeling in front of me, and I cup her head with my hand.

I gaze at her, wondering if a moment could be more perfect—that is, until she opens her mouth slightly and licks her lips.

I groan. That tongue. As soon as I saw it, I imagined how it would feel on me. She sits on her knees, tips back her head and opens her mouth. It's like she's begging me to fuck her mouth and it's the sexiest thing I've ever fucking seen.

I take a half step closer, grip her hair in my hand, and paint her lips with the head of my dick.

She makes a humming noise, the vibrations making me want to shout out loud. She's so fucking perfect and knows exactly how to get to the core of me. I take hold of the root of my dick and push into her mouth. Her eyes go wide and she slides her hands up the back of my thighs. Her lips close around my length, but she doesn't move. Our eyes lock, and I know what she's asking me. What she wants.

Fuck.

I slide in deeper. Her eyes are on me, watering slightly as I get to the back of her throat. She swallows and I groan at the sensation, pulling back slightly.

She moves, taking me in deeper still, then reaches for my hand in her hair, asking for more.

This woman.

My eyes close for a long beat as I try to compose myself, but there's something in me that can't hold back with her. I grip her hair tighter and pull back.

"You want me to fuck your mouth?" I ask. "That's what you want?"

She nods, her eyes soft. Submissive. When I know she's anything but.

I clench my jaw and push back into her, a little rougher. Not just because she's asked for it, but because I can't hold back anymore.

Her gagging noises run into moans of pleasure. My entire body tightens.

Fuck.

Fuck.

Fuck.

I want to stretch out this moment and make it last for days. I want her on her knees in front of me, her mouth around my cock, for the rest of time. I want to be seventy and replay this scene in my head over and over again.

She makes a low humming sound that vibrates at the back of her mouth, and I push deeper, chasing each second of sensation.

My orgasm grumbles in the distance. It's gaining ground and I pull out with a grunt. Her eyes don't leave mine as she sticks out her tongue. She knows what's next.

Her fingernails dig into my ass, and I grip the base of my cock and erupt over her wet, warm tongue, pulsing thick white ropes of come all over her.

I think I may have met my match.

SEVENTEEN

Bennett

She emerges from the shower wrapped in a towel that's far too big. I can't see enough skin.

"What's today got in store for us?" she asks. I'm still lying in bed, my hand tucked behind my head as I watch her every move.

"My vote is for you dropping that towel and getting over here."

She flicks her towel open and shuts it again, and I can't help but laugh at her flashing me.

"I didn't catch that. Do it again."

"I vote for wood chopping and s'mores," she replies, ignoring my request for more naked Efa. "We have to make the most of our surroundings. We should build a fire and do campfire-y stuff."

"Like s'mores."

"And we can sing songs."

And fuck in the moonlight, I think to myself. I can focus

on the physical and ignore the fact that I enjoy Efa almost as much in clothes as I do out of them.

I push back the covers and jump to my feet. "Okay, I brought a plaid shirt with me. I'm ready to be a mountaineer."

"Hmm, sounds like I need some help from a hunky lumberjack. If you find a number, let me know. In the meantime, dig out that plaid shirt and let's go chop some wood."

I laugh and head to the bathroom. It takes me five minutes to make it from the bed to the door of the cabin, dressed in my plaid shirt.

"Efa," I call and head out to the deck. Did that girl start without me? I dread to think the damage she could do with a sharp axe. "Efa!"

"Did someone call?" she replies and walks into my eyeline.

She's wearing the cowboy hat that was hanging on the porch, sunglasses, my walking boots, and nothing else but a white bra and matching panties. And she's got an axe over her shoulder.

I'm pretty sure every teenage boy in America would pay for the view I have right now.

"Can I get photographs of this?" I call.

She turns around in a circle, showing off her bare ass in her thong. When she's facing me again, she puts her free hand on her hip. "I'm ready for action. Come show me how to do manly wood-chopping things."

"I'm not going anywhere near an axe when you're dressed like that. I'll cut off my own hand."

"Hmmm." She taps her finger against her chin as if she's thinking about solutions that don't involve her going inside and getting dressed. "I guess I need your shirt, then." She smiles, pushing out a hip.

I pad down the wooden steps, unbuttoning my shirt, stripping as I stride toward her.

"Put some clothes on," I say, draping my shirt over her shoulders.

"First time you've ever said that." She hands me the axe and puts her hands through my shirtsleeves.

"First time you've ever wielded an axe."

My shirt hits her knees, and even though she's rolled up my shirtsleeves, they still go past her wrists.

She looks perfect.

The last thing I want to do right now is chop wood.

"So?" she says. "Where do we start? And honestly, like why? I get it if you want to chop down a tree, but whenever I see people chopping wood on Insta, it's already in little chunks. Why are they cutting it down again? It'll already fit on the fire."

I love how her brain works, how she sees gaps in logic without really looking for them. Even if she's wrong in this instance.

I grab the log from where she's placed it, ready to be split on the stump, and toss it back into the pile where she got it from. "Well, firstly, there's no way you're chopping anything wearing... nothing, even if you do now have my shirt on. And secondly, you split wood to speed up the drying process. Nothing we split now can be used right away." I head to the log stack on the porch. "These, on the other hand, have all been split and dried."

"But I want to do outdoorsy shit. Shouldn't we split some others so whoever comes next has dry firewood?"

"You're not dressed for outdoorsy shit, other than fucking on the porch. And I guarantee Worth has someone come in to make sure the cabin is set up for whoever's coming next."

She pouts a little and steps toward me, tracing her finger down my chest. "I have a lumberjack fantasy I was hoping to bring to life." She shifts her weight and looks up from under her lashes.

Never have I given in to a woman—to anyone—so easily.

"I'll split one piece of wood if you stay on the porch where you can't get hurt."

She tilts her head and a smile nudges the edge of her lips. She's won and she knows it.

"You got yourself a deal." She turns and shrugs off my shirt, but takes it with her. She leans against the post of the porch at the top of the steps.

I take back one of the logs from the pile and place it on the stump. Growing up in Hollywood, I didn't get much opportunity to split logs. Lucky for me, I've taken a few camping trips and learned the basics. I may not give Efa all the details of what has become a cringe-worthy phase in my history—I bought a truck and grew a beard, on top of changing my name—but I can give her a glimpse of one of the skills I learned during that off-the-rails time. I wanted to do every anti-Hollywood thing I could think of. And right now—thank god. I don't remember ever wanting to impress anyone as much as I do Efa in this moment.

"You're so fucking hot," she shouts, and I can't help but grin. She never second-guesses herself. It's so fucking refreshing.

"Back at you," I say, just before I bring the axe down, being careful to aim for the edges of the wood and not the middle, just as I've been taught. The blade slices through the wood, cleanly splitting the log in two.

Efa whoops from the sidelines, a one-woman cheer-leading team. I'm not ashamed to admit, it feels fucking great.

I put the bigger chunk of the log back on the stump and bring down the axe again and it splinters into two. I do the same with the other chunk. Job done.

"Have you ticked off your lumberjack fantasy now?" I call over to where she's still at the top of the porch steps.

She takes her hat off and tosses it onto the Adirondack behind her. "Now this is the bit where you get over here and fuck me on the porch," she says.

I wonder if there'll ever be a time when that's not the best offer on the table.

EIGHTEEN

Efa

We're sitting on the bank of the lake or pond or whatever the water is in front of us. All I know is that it's not the ocean. The sounds of birds and our intermittent voices are the only things I've heard all day. There's no traffic noise. No distant shouts of laughter. Nothing but peace.

Bennett is lying between my legs, where he's been most of the day, except at the moment we're both dressed and we're just sitting, my fingers twisting in his hair as we appreciate the hell out of the moment. The surface of the water is so smooth it looks like glass set over a landscape painting. Every now and then a bird takes off from a tree, making the leaves shiver, or a duck touches down in the water, sending ripples a short distance before they disappear. Everything stays the same and everything's just about to change.

The sun is low in the sky, and the light is all burnt orange and luminous. It feels like we're in a movie—like this moment is so perfect, it can't possibly be real.

"Today has been... magical," I say.

He nods, and I push my hand down the back of his neck and under the cotton of his t-shirt, wanting to share more of his warm skin against mine.

"You're great," I say.

He turns and looks me in the eye like he wants to say something, like it's hovering there, just beneath the surface. He hands me a smooth gray stone. "Can you skim stones?"

I shrug. "I've never tried."

"You can have your first time with me."

I know it's a joke, but his words tug on something inside me. Suddenly I'm aware that there's going to be a thousand first times for me in my future, and the best ones are going to be those I shared with Bennett.

I take the stone from him, his fingers sliding against mine, and we stand.

I'm only in New York for the summer, I remind myself.

Except that I have no particular reason to leave.

He looks at me, and I don't know if he can tell what I'm thinking, but he dips his head and kisses me. "Hold it like this," he says. "You want it to slice through the surface of the water and bounce."

"Show me," I say.

He launches his stone and it hops on the surface of the water, once, twice, three times—four—then plunges into the lake.

He grins back at me. "It's so satisfying and I have no idea why."

"Let me try." I pull back my arm and try to aim it the same way he did. To my surprise, the stone hits the water and bounces. But only once.

"You did it," he says, offering up his palm for a high five.

I give him one.

"What kind of stones are good for skimming?" I crouch to start sifting through what's on the ground.

"Flat, smooth, medium size and weight."

We start combing the shore, picking up stones that might work. The ones on the surface are still warm, retaining the rays of the sun they've collected throughout the day.

"Okay, so what about these?" I stand and he comes over to inspect my pickings.

A couple he discards, which leaves me three. "These should work."

"Let me see yours," I say.

He opens his hand to reveal three pale gray stones and a black one. I reach for the black one.

"This is shaped like a heart," I say. "You can't throw that into the lake." I hold it up to the fading light.

"You want to take it home?" he asks almost teasingly, like there's something wrong with taking a stone home from a trip to the lake.

I drop it into his shirt pocket. "Yeah. Keep it safe."

Our eyes lock together, and this time it's like we're both not saying what we're thinking. *This moment is perfect. Today has been perfect. Let's do it all over tomorrow and the next day and the next day.*

"You're great," I say, realizing only as the words echo in my own ears that I've already told him that. I feel stupid. I don't want him to think I'm asking for anything, because I'm not.

He presses his lips to mine. "You're great too."

"And I'm pleased I ran into you, even if it meant I can't ever work for Fort Inc." I grin and expect him to laugh, but he doesn't.

"You've accepted that?" he asks.

"Yes," I reply. "Even though trying to get a job at Fort was a big reason why I came to New York. But you were clear and... now... I don't want to get a job and always wonder if I'm there because I'm fantastic in bed."

He laughs.

"But seriously, you should know that I choose you over the job any day of the week." The words could be brushed off as nothing. He could make a joke about how the sex between us is addictive or explosive or any of the other things it definitely is.

But I don't mean that I would choose *sex* with him over the job. I mean, I choose *him*. Hanging out. Talking. Being. With. Him.

And he knows it too.

His stare warms me from the inside out, and I know there's so much he doesn't say. I don't push him. I don't want what's not freely given. Not a job, not his heart.

He cups my face in his hands and presses his mouth against mine in a chaste but passionate kiss that leaves me breathless and wanting.

NINETEEN

Bennett

Worth's dining table would seat twenty people. I'm sitting at one end, on the phone to my head of security, Aarvi, while Efa takes a shower.

"What's the latest?" I ask.

"Something's happened," Aarvi says. "We're not sure how, but they seem to have gotten access to an encrypted part of the systems. No one's ever done that before."

It feels like whoever it is, they're closing in.

"They were in for a second before another layer of security kicked in. They won't have gotten anything."

"You think it's the same source targeting us each time?"

"It's all the time, and yes, I think it's coming from one source."

"You think it's my identity they're after or something else?" I've asked this question of Aarvi before and she always gives me the same answer. Doesn't stop me asking.

"I think if someone just wanted to disclose your identity, they could bribe a member of staff. It's not like there haven't been photographs of you out there. It's not someone looking for who you are. It's Fort they want."

It makes sense this time, just like all the times she's said it before. I don't know why I still feel like *I'm* being hunted.

"So you think they want details of Project Next Generation?" We're working on groundbreaking AI tech—highly confidential. We don't want it getting into the wrong hands before we have the right checks and balances in place.

"Everyone who has even heard a whisper of it wants details."

"We need to build in more security," I say.

"Already done. I'm implementing the security plan I sent you."

"I don't like that they got in. Even if it was for a second."

Efa slides her hand over my back. I look up and pull her down onto my lap, trying to ignore her bare thighs and the way her already short skirt rides up as she balances on my knee. She lays her head on my shoulder as Aarvi and I discuss other strategies for keeping the walls at Fort strong. Aarvi is all over it, and her plan doesn't require second-guessing. Fort is in good hands, but I wonder if there's someone out there even better who's going to crash into our systems. Are we just sitting ducks?

Efa presses a kiss just below my ear, and I know my phone call is about to come to an end.

"So you'll send me a revised report?" I ask.

"By close of business today. And if anything else happens, you'll be the first to know."

I end the call and bring my attention to Efa. I pull her across my lap so she's sitting astride me.

"Hey," I say. "You smell nice."

"All clean. That rain shower is incredible." She wraps her arms around my neck, pushing her fingers through my hair. Being with her over these last few days has been... eye-opening. I'm more relaxed around her. Happier, even. It's good to be out of the city, with nothing to focus on but each other.

"I can get you dirty again if you want an excuse to make the most of it," I say.

She shifts and our bodies lock together like we came out of the same mold. She circles her hips, pressing against the denim of my jeans. I think she's about to kiss me, but instead she changes tack completely—something I'm coming to expect from her.

"You know, you should really focus on tracking down who's coming for you. You've got a real defensive strategy—and I'm sure it's the best defensive strategy there is. But it's like you're waiting around for an attack. You need to take the fight to the hacker."

It's difficult to concentrate when she's grinding against my dick, but what she's saying makes sense. It echoes my own fears, that we're just biding our time until the other shoe drops.

"We've tried to. They're covering their tracks well. As you'd expect." I'm not sure *how* hard we've tried. Efa's right —we've been focused on making sure they don't get through. We've been building higher walls rather than trying to find who's slamming into them with a virtual battering ram. I've been more about keeping a low profile than really trying to turn the tables and figure out who's behind the attacks.

She sighs and drops a kiss at the corner of my mouth. "Let me try, will you? I want to see if I can figure out where the attacks are coming from."

I chuckle. "You think you can outsmart the brightest brains in the business?"

She shrugs. "Maybe. Or maybe I'll just offer a different perspective. See something new because I'm an outsider."

Thankfully I don't have to tell her no, because my phone pings behind Efa on the dining table. I grab it in case it's important.

It's just Leo.

"Fuck," I say, and Efa stops pressing kisses against my jaw and pulls back.

"Leo," I say. "He wants his new girlfriend to come to our Monday night thing."

"Monday? I've forgotten what day it is."

"It's Friday. We leave tomorrow."

"And Monday is No Girls Allowed?" she asks.

"It's not that. It's just, this girl came out of nowhere. Last I heard, he'd seen her a few nights running. Now he has a girlfriend? Leo never falls like this. I don't know. There's something off about it."

"Sounds terrible," Efa says, trailing a finger down my chest and finding the button of my jeans. "But maybe she's just what Leo needs." She takes my hand and places it under her skirt, between her legs. Our eyes lock as my fingers touch bare flesh.

She's not wearing panties.

What am I worrying about Leo for? I have a hot, half-naked woman in my lap.

My fingers press into her folds, and she gasps like it's the first time she's ever felt me there. "I can't get enough of you," I say on a groan as she unzips my jeans and pulls out my cock.

I'm already hard.

Already ready for her.

I'm always ready.

For more.

"Tell Leo you're going to bring me on Monday night," she says breathlessly as I circle her clit with my thumb. "I can chat to the girlfriend while you get to have alone time with the boys. See if I pick up bad vibes."

"Yes," I grunt. I don't know what I'm saying yes to. The way her hand grips my cock? Her inviting herself Monday night?

All of it.

All of her.

TWENTY

Efa

There aren't many places I don't bring my laptop, but meeting Bennett's friends should be one of them. Instead, I've slipped my computer into my tote like I'm heading to the library to work on some code.

After hassling Bennett to put me in touch with his head of security as soon as we got back from the Catskills a couple of days ago, I've been rooting around, trying to find patterns in the security breaches. Trying to put the information together so it makes sense. I've been trying to figure stuff out.

Luckily for me, Bennett has been stuck working since we got back—his penance for a midweek break, he said. I've gotten some time alone, which has meant I can work as well. If Bennett had been here, I'm sure I would have been naked all day.

My body's grateful for the break. Every part of me is tender, but I can't ever say no to Bennett. I don't want to.

"You okay?" He squeezes my hand as we head up the steps of the brownstone.

"Yes. Should I not be?" I grin at him.

"You don't need to be nervous."

I laugh. "I'm not. If these guys are your friends, I'm sure they'll be welcoming and charming. I'm going to love them."

He knocks on the door. "You're not concerned that they might not like you?"

"Should I be? Of course they'll like me. Americans always like the British."

"Tell that to seventeen seventy-six."

I laugh and he grins at me—not because he's amused by his own joke, but because he's happy he made me laugh. My joy brings him happiness and that gives me a sense of peace that I've never known before.

I met him just a few weeks ago, but I understand Bennett on a level I never expected. And he gets me like we've always been meant to be together—it's just taken a little while to find each other.

"You brought your laptop?" he says, peering into my tote.

I shrug, trying to act like it's no big deal. The fact is, I'm really hoping to have a chance to do a bit of investigating into Bennett's cyber stalker-slash-hacker. Surprisingly for a man with Bennett's power and responsibility, he's really good at ignoring his phone when we're together. I'm willing to bet he's the same with his friends. It's just a hunch, but Bennett not looking at his phone for a period of time each week would be a good opportunity for a malware attack on Fort through Bennett's phone. Malware attacks can slow up a phone, so Bennett would know something was up if there was an attack while he was active on his device.

It's a long shot, but I have little else to go on. I just don't want to tell Bennett. I have a feeling he wouldn't take it well. The only people who know he's not looking at his phone during these Monday night get-togethers are his five friends—the ones he trusts with his life.

I don't have to explain myself, because the door unlocks and a tall guy with geek glasses and long hair pushed back over his ears, opens the door.

"Wow, Bennett," I say. "Your friends are hot."

Bennett rolls his eyes. "Worth, this is Efa."

I hold out my hand in formal greeting, but Worth pulls me in for a hug. "Delighted to meet the woman who keeps this guy on a leash."

"Oh it's the other way around," I reply. "I'm always on all fours around him."

Worth barks out a laugh and beckons us inside.

We're shown downstairs to the basement. It's got a bar area at one end and a huge screen on the other, with comfy-looking velvet chairs arranged in stadium rows. A couple of guys are gathered around the large black bar. The entire room has a moody vibe, and I don't need to ask whether Worth's married. He's definitely a bachelor with décor like this.

We're given drinks and I'm introduced to Jack and Fisher as we stand by the bar. They're both hot, but if I have to put them in any kind of hotness order, which of course I do, I'd have to put Bennett at the top, with Worth coming up behind as a close second.

"Byron isn't coming, so we're just waiting for Leo," Worth says.

"Waiting for Leo?" Bennett says. "When does that ever happen?" No doubt, that's his new girlfriend's fault. Bennett sounds like a jealous ex. I slide my hand into his, hoping it will calm him.

What's his problem? Is it the change that's the issue? Does he hate the idea that anybody could be added to these sacrosanct Monday nights? Does he not like sharing Leo's attention?

"You're from London, I hear," Jack says, pulling my attention away from Bennett's reaction. "It's my favorite city. Particularly when Leo and Fisher are in New York."

"Nothing beats it," I say.

"Not even New York with this uptight asshole in it?" Jack asks, nodding at Bennett.

I laugh. "You're saying that like it would improve New York's chances. There's a reason Bennett isn't front and center of New York's tourist board advertising campaign."

Jack chuckles.

"I'm offended," Bennett deadpans, and I can't help but laugh at his sarcasm.

"Sounds like she's gotten to know you pretty well," Jack says.

"Oh hey—thanks for letting us stay at your beautiful place in the Catskills," I say to Worth. "We had the best time."

"No problem. I like to get up there as often as I can."

"I told her that's where you like to bury the bodies," Bennett says.

"Great location," I say. "Such a choice of burial sites."

"Oh my god, you two are made for each other," Jack says. "I've never met anyone with a sense of humor as dark as Bennett's."

I grin. "I have an older brother who was quite the emo in his day. Gallows humor doesn't scare me."

The doorbell goes and Worth moves away from our group to answer it. I wonder if I'm going to get the chance to disappear and run the tests I really want to while all these guys are together.

There's something weird about the most recent attacks on Fort. I'm not sure Bennett's team has picked up on the shift, but recently they have fallen into a fairly predictable pattern. They seem to escalate at the same time each week. And they get more aggressive each time, coming progressively closer to breaking through the firewalls.

It happens every seven days—although it doesn't look like that at first. You have to dig deeper, but when you do, it's clear the attack is on some kind of cycle—not unlike Bennett's catch-up with his mates on Monday nights. I just want to flip open my laptop and see if there's anything lurking, waiting to pounce on Bennett's phone.

"What's the time?" Jack asks. "Does this thing actually work?" He nods at the screen at the other end of the room. "Or is it there to look pretty?"

Worth comes through with two people who I assume are Leo and his girlfriend.

"It works," Worth says. He's clearly overheard Jack moaning. "Stop bitching." He slips behind the bar.

"I'm Efa," I say to Leo's girlfriend. She's beautiful—like, straight from a catwalk, legs for days, green eyes with extra-long lashes, and blonde hair that sweeps back like she's in front of a wind machine.

"Hi." She leans forward and air-kisses me on both cheeks. "I'm Nadia," she says. "Leo's girlfriend."

"Let's sit," Bennett says. "You don't want to watch sports, do you?" he asks me.

I know I'm here to keep Nadia out of Bennett's way. And I'm happy to help. "Nadia and I can catch up by the bar," I say. "As long as you have snacks, Worth? Tell me you have a bucketload of carbs for me."

He grins and pulls out packets of kettle chips, corn chips, popcorn, and pretzels. "Worth, are you single?" I ask. "Because I just became extremely attracted to you."

Bennett bends and kisses me on the head. The boys head to the chairs while Nadia and I take seats on barstools.

"So how did you meet Leo?" I ask Nadia.

She shrugs. "A party. A friend of mine was opening a club." Her eyes flit to the door. "I'm just going to pop to the ladies' room." She pats me on the hand, takes her phone and slides off her stool.

I peek over at Bennett. As I suspected, his phone is nowhere to be seen. He glances over at me and I blow him a kiss. I swear I catch the beginnings of a blush before the TV snags his attention. I'm not even going to pretend to be interested. I can barely cope with the rules of sports I've grown up with; I'm not going to start to learn weird American games.

Nadia is taking her time. I hope she's okay in there. I'm just about to take my phone out and text Eira when she reappears.

"Has it started?" she asks me.

I nod. "I think so."

"Shall we go and sit?" she asks.

"Oh, I thought we could chat?" I say. "Are you from New York?"

She glances between me and Leo. I'm not sure I'm going to be very helpful keeping her attention away from him for the evening. She seems super keen to be physically close with him.

"Russia," she says.

"Oh!" I reply. "I didn't detect an accent."

She shrugs, her eyes pinned on the screen now. She's

not interested in me. "I've been modeling so long, I guess I lost it."

"Oh fun. You're a model?" I ask, stuffing two corn chips in my mouth.

"Yeah, I still do some."

"And that's why you came to New York?" I ask her, desperate to keep her attention for as long as I can. "I'd never been before this trip. It's a great city."

"It's a great city if you have money," she says. "Otherwise it's a shit city."

Her aggressive tone catches me off guard. I can't think of what to say.

"Baby, I miss you," she croons over to Leo. Apparently he doesn't hear her, and her mouth sets in a hard line. She turns back to me. "You think we should go over?"

She really has no interest in getting to know me at all. I can't exactly pin her to the barstool. "I'm going to stay here," I say. "Bennett gets so little time with his friends, I don't want to impose."

Her eyes linger on me longer than before. They flit down my body, like she's taking me in, then she looks away. "Yeah. You're right."

If she did go and sit with Leo, I might get a chance to open my laptop—but then Bennett would be miserable. No matter what happens on the TV, tonight's going to be a losing game. For me at least.

TWENTY-ONE

Efa

As I push my key into the lock, Bennett's hands slide over my hips from behind and his lips find my neck. I managed to keep Nadia from going to sit on Leo's lap for forty-five minutes. And as much as I would have loved to have stayed at the bar and tried to discover any attacks on Fort through Bennett's phone, it would have looked weird if I'd stayed on my own. So I joined them, and Bennett did his best not to snarl at Nadia. I'm proud of him.

I don't know why I bothered to take my laptop. It was never going to work out. And it was only a hunch. There's no conclusive evidence of where the attacks are coming from. That's the problem.

"They loved you," he growls. "You fit in so perfectly. Like you were their little sister or something."

"That get you hot?" I turn and face him, and he braces his hands either side of my door. "That I'm your best friend's little sister?" I angle my head up and lick along the seam of his lips. "You shouldn't touch me, but you just can't keep your hands off me." I reach down to feel him and he's already hard.

He's always hard.

"I definitely can't keep my hands off you."

I face the door again and, this time, turn the key so we can get into the flat before this turns into something more than a PG groping.

"You managed to control yourself, unlike Nadia." I kick the door closed and giggle, remembering the way she practically latched herself to Leo most of the night. "You think she was a cat in a previous life?" She spent a lot of the evening licking Leo's ear. "No kink-shaming intended."

Bennett groans. "Way to kill my boner."

I laugh. "However old they get, men are always fifteen-year-old boys at heart. At least she seems genuinely into him."

"You think?" Bennett asks. "You don't think it's a bit much?"

"You think she should be a bit meaner to him? Like I am to you?" I hook my finger into his belt and pull him down onto the sofa with me.

"It just felt a bit forced. A bit fake. You think she's after his money?" he asks.

"I mean, that's part of the package, I suppose. But is saying that she's using him for his money any worse than saying he's using her because she gives a good blow job?"

"Is that what she told you? That he likes the way she gives head?"

"Of course not. I'm just talking in hypotheticals. It's too simplistic to say someone's only with that person for the money. It's a package. On both sides." I shrug. "Except you. I'm just using you for your big dick, in case you didn't know already."

"I did know that," he says. "But seriously. Something didn't feel off to you?"

I've never seen Bennett agitated like he is now. I don't understand how his mate's girlfriend could be the person to cause such agitation.

"She's gorgeous," I say, holding up my thumb. "She's clearly into him." I extend a finger. "They clearly have sexual chemistry—we were all subjected to the evidence of that." I extend a third finger.

"But do you think they laugh?" he asks. "Like we do?"

Something tugs in my chest at the way he's holding us up as the bar for what a happy couple should look like.

"I don't know," I say honestly. "Maybe. If it works for both of them, what does it matter? If she'll give him what he wants, who cares if she enjoys his money?"

"It just makes me itch."

"He's probably going to be richer than most of the women he dates. Doesn't mean that's all they see in him. If you're friends with him, he must have some redeeming qualities other than his money."

Bennett's lost in thought and I lay my head on his shoulder. "You're protective of him. I get it."

"I've seen users before. Hangers-on. Sycophants." He spits out the words with the venom of someone who's been used. Or had a mother who was.

"They're everywhere," I agree, threading my fingers through his. "But what can you do? If you tell him you think his girlfriend's using him, you're going to lose a friend."

"Sometimes I fantasize about revenge on those people who only came around when my mother was riding high. They weren't there when she got dropped by a director for putting on ten pounds or when she missed the Oscar nomination for *Homecoming*."

I love that he's so protective and caring about his mother, but sad that he's so eaten up by this. "Fame. Money. It attracts the worst of the world."

He grunts in response.

"But all beautiful things in this world attract darkness. That's the way life is."

"Maybe. But Hollywood is full of the worst of humanity. You know even her agent of thirty years dropped her when she got sick?"

I curl into him, burrowing into his neck. He still feels the sting all these years later.

"Is it awful that sometimes I think it's better that she died young? Because aging as an actress never goes well. Your career nosedives and no one wants to know you."

"Did you ever want to go into acting?"

He shakes his head. "She never pushed me in that direction, either. And she never made me walk the red carpet. I never did photoshoots with her—you know, like some stars love to have their entire family in *Vanity Fair*? There was none of that."

"Sounds like she was as protective of you as you are of her, even now."

He sighs. "As much as she could be in that environment."

I pause, waiting for him to say what he *wasn't* protected from, but he doesn't elaborate. "What do you mean, as much as she could be?"

He shakes his head and takes a breath, his chest expanding under me, his warmth multiplying. I press a kiss to his pectoral muscle, over his shirt. "Nothing specific, but her fame did impact me. She couldn't help it. Kids at school wanted to be my friend because of who my mom was. And then they didn't want to be my friend because of who my mom was."

"That's horrible," I say.

"It doesn't matter. I have real people around me now." He brings my hand up to his mouth and kisses the inside of my wrist, then pulls me onto his lap. "Did you have a good time tonight?"

"I did," I say, but when I meet his eye, I know it's not just me that catches the hesitancy in my voice.

"But?" he asks.

I shrug. "You say you've known all these guys since business school and you're close with them all. Even Leo?"

He narrows his eyes like he's trying to read between the lines of what I'm saying. "Yeah. Especially Leo." His stare carries an edge of warning.

I'm pushing, but the door is closed.

"That's good." I nod.

I want his friends to be as loyal as he thinks they are. I really do. I'm just not convinced.

"It *is* good. I don't doubt any of them." The tension sheets us like thick fog, and none of it is sexual. "You're lucky," I say.

"Very," he says. "I've known them all a very long time."

I'd known my uncle my entire life and look how he betrayed me. But I don't say it. I don't need to. Bennett isn't an idiot, and if he believes that his friends are entirely loyal to him, there's no point in suggesting anything else. Not until I have more than a gut feeling and a couple of days with my laptop. I need more.

TWENTY-TWO

Efa

The hotel doesn't need me today, so I'm making the most of my time off by catching up on missed sleep. I don't know what time Bennett left this morning, but he left an apple on the pillow for my breakfast, so I didn't even need to get out of bed.

I take a bite and my phone goes. It's my sister and thank god it's not a video call.

"Hey," I say as I answer.

"You're not working," she says.

"They don't need me. Apparently the vomiting bug has passed. And the weather got really hot. I don't think they're as busy as they expected."

"Good for you, I guess. Any luck getting an interview at Fort?"

I wish I'd never told her that I'd made some progress. I'd just been so shocked to have stumbled upon Ben Fort, I had to tell somebody *something*.

"No. Fort by name and fort by nature," I say. "They

wouldn't even admit that Fort was in the building when I asked at reception."

"What, they pretended they were the FBI or something?" she asks.

"It's a mixed-use building. They just said that they don't have any record of Fort in the building."

"Wow, so they just lie?"

"I guess." My gut churns a little. I set my apple down on the bedside table and sit up so I'm against the headboard.

"And how's this Bennett guy? Are you still seeing him?"

"Yes," I say, in the best fake-breezy tone I can muster. "I mean, obviously it's casual."

"Didn't you just go away for a weekend?"

"Yeah, to the Catskills. It was beautiful. Completely in the middle of nowhere."

"That doesn't sound casual to me. Tell me about him."

I snuggle back down the bed, catching Ben's scent in the pillow next to me. "He's kind," I say. "And tall. Like, he's at least as tall as Dax. He's a little grumpy. Not to me, but he's not a big people person."

"Right. Sounds delightful."

"He is," I say. "Well, maybe *delightful* isn't the word I'd use exactly, but... I have fun with him and he makes me laugh." I don't want her to hate him, even though on first impressions he might not come off as the pussycat my sister might want for me.

"What does he do for a living? He does have a job, doesn't he?"

I groan inwardly at the thought of having to lie to Eira. What am I meant to say? Make up a story for my sister? I want to tell her every single detail about Bennett. "He's in tech," I say.

"Wow, that's a coincidence," she says.

"Not really. He's into the hardware. Processers and stuff, you know?"

She laughs. "No, not really. What's his surname? I'll Google him. See who we're dealing with."

I wince. What am I going to say? I shouldn't have to lie to my sister. Or even half-lie.

"Oh, he's not on the internet. He's really... private."

"What do you mean, he's not on the internet. Is that even a thing?"

It is if you're Bennett Fordham, I don't say.

"He just doesn't like people knowing his business."

"Eddie!" she gasps. "Is he a criminal?"

"Of course he's not a criminal," I say.

"Then tell me his name."

My brain is clunking in my head, trying to figure out how I can stop my sister thinking Bennett is a mob boss while not betraying him.

But why would talking to my sister about the man I'm sleeping with be a betrayal? It's ludicrous that I can't talk to her about him. I talk to her about everything.

"I can't," I say. "I'm sorry, Eira."

Silence echoes on the other end of the line.

"It's fine," she says finally. But I know it's not, and I hate the fact that she's pretending to be okay. Because it's not okay. We don't have secrets between us. Bennett shouldn't be the first. "Does this mystery tech man at least know someone at Fort who could get you in?"

"No. Apparently, Ben Fort makes all recruitment decisions himself, and he handpicks from a pool of candidates recommended by people who already work there. I don't have much chance. But there are plenty of tech companies in the US. I just need to cast my net a little wider."

I feel like such a liar.

"Sounds like you just need to find someone who works at Fort and get a recommendation."

And not sleep with Ben Fort, thus rendering yourself ineligible for a position. But the truth is, I don't regret sleeping with him and giving up on my dream to work for Fort Inc. How can I?

"Yeah, it's not so easy. People aren't allowed to disclose they work for Fort."

"What? Like they're spies or something?"

I laugh. It's as ridiculous as she's making it sound. I don't have any defense on Bennett's behalf.

"I think I'm just going to get over my Fort obsession and find a different horse to ride. I'm sure I'd learn a lot if I worked at Google or Microsoft or somewhere."

"I thought the entire point of going to Fort is that it's small enough that you'd be able to try lots of different things."

I sigh. "That was an advantage, but I have to accept that it's not going to happen for me."

"You want me to get Vincent to ask around for you?"

"Eira, you've promised you're going to try and not be so interfering."

"I'm just trying to help. The Coves are a well-connected, successful family. And they're our family now. There's nothing wrong with asking family for help."

"But none of them are in tech."

"I think Vincent has a tech company."

I sigh. "I don't want to get a job because of who I know. I want to deserve the job and get it because of that."

The silence from the other end of the phone tells me Eira doesn't agree with me. But there's a reason Bennett doesn't employ people he sleeps with. It's no coincidence that he's called the man with the Midas touch. He makes decisions based on data, not friendships and favors.

Although it hasn't helped him catch his hacker. "Oh, actually maybe the Cove mafia might be able to help me with something," I say. "Do any of them know someone who could help with tech security?"

"You're looking for some work experience or something?"

"Maybe," I say. "I've just gotten a little more into it. It's a growth area I might want to explore."

"Hang on a minute."

The phone goes dead—she's muted me, which is a sure sign she's either having a conversation with her soon-to-be husband or she's peeing.

"I knew it," she says a few seconds later. "You know Sutton's best friend, Parker?"

I try to think. "Sutton is Jacob's wife, right? Brother-in-law number one?"

"Right. Her best friend is married to a hacker. Is that right, Dax?" she calls out. "Yes, Dax says he's some kind of famous hacker. Can hack anything. Has worked on all sorts of stuff for governments."

He sounds like the exact person I need to help me figure out what's going on at Fort—the exact person Bennett would use if he trusted anyone outside his business.

"I'm not sure he's got an office you could do work experience at, but maybe he knows someone."

"Can you introduce me?" I ask. "By email. I'd like to talk to him ASAP if possible."

"He might know someone at Fort," she suggests.

"Maybe," I say. "It would be great to speak to him. Thanks, Eira."

"Now who's interfering?" she asks.

"It's not interfering if I *ask* for help."

She sighs. "Whatever. I'll get Dax to do the intro since I don't know the guy very well. Only met him once or twice."

"That would be great, thanks. And for the record, you're so much better at not interfering now than you used to be."

"Putting that on a t-shirt. 'Not as interfering as I used to be.'"

"Christmas present sorted."

She laughs. It's a sound I always cherish. Eira had it tough after my parents died. Seeing her so happy now, makes *me* so happy.

"Next time you call, you think we'll get to see this Bennett of yours?" she asks.

My stomach twists, because I know Bennett's never going to want to appear on a video call with my sister. He wouldn't want to risk it. The last few weeks, I've enjoyed our bubble, just the two of us hiding out from the world. But if we can't manage lunch at Shake Shack, or a video call with my sister, it doesn't say much for the possibility that he and I might exist for more than a New York minute. And if being with him means I have to live a life where I'm lying to my sister... that doesn't work for me.

I didn't come here to find anyone. And even though Bennett definitely feels like the kind of someone I'd like to find, the man who will ultimately take up space in my life can't force me to hide from the world—or even just my sister. Sooner or later, the bubble is going to burst.

TWENTY-THREE

Bennett

I'm not sure how it's possible to look as gorgeous as she does wrapped up in a towel. "Wanna get dirty again?"

"I have to get to work, otherwise obviously the answer is yes."

"Tonight, then?" I stand in front of the mirror, towel around my waist, shaving cream on my face.

"I'll be back by five," she says. "I'm in housekeeping today."

"I have meetings until six."

"You're going back to the hotel now? How ironic that despite your suite, you sleep here and work there," she says. As she passes me in the bathroom, she stops and presses a kiss on my arm. My skin fizzes underneath her lips. Every part of her feels good.

I've never spent this much time with a woman, never woken up and gotten dressed with someone before. It feels better than natural. It's fun and comforting and *more* than I might have imagined. Not that I ever imagined myself here. I've always considered myself a loner.

"I'm going to call Eira tonight. Guinevere has had a temperature, so I just want to check everything's okay."

"Okay." Do I know who Guinevere is? I'm sure I would have remembered the name if she'd mentioned it before. "Who's Guinevere?" I ask.

"My niece," she replies from the bedroom.

I don't know if I'm imagining things, but it feels like the air between us has shifted a little. "Are you mad I didn't know who Guinevere is?" I ask.

"No," she snaps. "I've never mentioned Guinevere before. Why would I be angry that you didn't know who she was?"

"You seem mad about something."

I turn and she's standing in the doorway to the bathroom, wearing nothing but panties and a bra. It's my favorite outfit of hers.

"You look beautiful," I say. "Are you going to be servicing my room today?"

"What can I tell my sister about you?" she asks, ignoring my question.

"Why do you have to tell your sister anything about me?" I reply, bringing the razor to my face.

"Because we're spending time together. We just went away for the weekend together. I just met five of your closest friends—"

"My only friends."

"Right," she says. "And they can know everything about *me*."

I try and relax my jaw, and when it doesn't work, I put the razor down. I'm pretty sure sharp objects should be out of reach right now. "Right," I reply.

"Can I tell her you're Ben Fort?"

My eyes slice to hers. She knows the answer to that. "That's not my name. My name is Bennett Fordham."

"And what is it you do, Bennett Fordham? Because I thought you were a self-made tech billionaire and president of Fort Inc."

I sigh. I was having such a nice morning. Shower sex followed by an incredible blow job. And now... this.

"I don't know what you want me to say."

"There's never going to be a time when I can be honest with my family about who you are, is there?" she asks.

I completely abandon my attempt at shaving and wipe the soap from my jaw with a towel. "I don't know what you're asking me. I haven't thought about... any of that. You know how careful I am about separating Bennett Fordham and Ben Fort."

She glances down at the floor, then turns and heads back into the bedroom.

Fuck.

I hate that I've upset her. I wasn't prepared for this conversation. At all. Maybe I'm naïve but it didn't occur to me that she needed or wanted to talk about me to anyone. It feels like it's been just the two of us for weeks now. No one else has been involved.

Until Monday night, when I took her to meet my friends.

I head into the bedroom to try to make things right. She's dressed and is just putting on her sneakers. "I'll see you later," she says and stands.

"Efa."

She turns to me. "What?"

Nothing I can say is going to make her feel better. I

don't want anyone knowing who I am. That's not going to change.

She waits for a beat, then two, then she turns and leaves.

Fuck, fuck, fuck.

TWENTY-FOUR

Efa

I can't believe I'm hanging out with a guy who managed to hack the CIA at sixteen. My luck changed right around midday today. Cleaning angry apparently means that everything gets done at warp speed, so I had my rooms done in record time. I managed to swap the Park Suite for one of the junior suites because one of the other girls was complaining about the guest and I offered to take it for her. I've not seen or heard from Bennett all day.

But what can he say? Nothing. He doesn't want me to reveal his identity to my family. To anyone. Being with him means I have to hide, too.

I ruminated for approximately five hours, until the Cove mafia finally did their thing and I got a message from my sister-in-law's best friend's husband, Tristan. The hacker.

And that's when my mood picked up.

He's in New York after a wedding and offered to meet up. Now, here we are. Just casually hanging out like it's no big deal.

"I can see the attacks happening. They definitely got in through a mobile device," Tristan says. "I can see it in the code."

"Can you see *which* mobile device?" I ask. I'd put money on it being Bennett's.

"Yup. I just need to get a number for it."

"Let me make you a tea," I say.

"Music to my ears coming from a British person. The Americans can't make tea." Tristan's phone bleeps and he starts typing. "I'm texting Parker your address. She's done at the Frick. Is that okay?"

"Of course. I'd love to meet her. Is she okay with you being here? Aren't you meant to be on holiday?"

"She knows I can't resist something like this. She's fine. We're staying at the Mandarin Oriental, so she'll basically pick me up on the way."

"The Mandarin Oriental is in the Deutsche Bank Center, isn't it?" I get up from the sofa and start to make tea.

"Yeah. You've been?"

"That's where Fort's offices are, but no, I've never been."

"So how did you get dragged into looking into Fort security? You'd think they'd have the best and the brightest on it."

I laugh. "You're assuming I'm not either?"

Tristan chuckles. "No offense meant. I know from Parker you don't work at Fort. She said you just graduated."

"Yeah. I don't work for them, as much as I'd like to."

"Oh, so this is about proving yourself, maybe getting your foot in the door?"

"No. I'm resigned to the fact I'm not going to work for Fort. I just really want to fix this issue. I have a friend who works there and it's..." I shrug. "It's causing him stress."

We lock eyes for a second. Tristan inherently under-stands that I can't say more and he doesn't push. "Well, if I can't figure it out, no one can."

"That's your reputation."

There's a knock at the door.

"That will be Parker," Tristan says.

But she would be rung up by the doorman, I think. I'm pretty sure I'm going to open the door to Bennett. At least, I hope I will. I hope he's come back. As much as I'm frus-trated at the situation, about his choices around his identity, it doesn't make me like him less. I've only known him a few weeks, but somehow, it feels like I had a Bennett-shaped hole in my heart and he's slotted right in.

I pass Tristan his tea and go to the door. Bennett stands in the doorway, his hair disheveled, like he's had a lot on his mind today. He just looks at me, his expression half sorrow, half pain.

"Hey," I say.

"I'm sorry," he replies.

"I got it," Tristan says from behind us.

Bennett glances behind me and sees Tristan. He frowns, turning his attention back to me. His expression is anger, disappointment, and confusion all rolled into one. He's jealous. He doesn't know who Tristan is and he's assumed the worst.

As if I could move on so quickly. We've not had conver-sations about tomorrow, let alone when I go back to England, but whatever happens, I could never just move on to the next guy like Bennett is nothing.

I reach for him at the same moment my buzzer goes.

"That will be Tristan's wife," I say, looking pointedly at Bennett. Without looking away from him, I call, "Tristan,

Parker's here." I answer the buzz and instruct the doorman to let her up.

"Tristan, this is my friend." I open the door to allow Bennett to introduce himself.

"Hi. Bennett Fordham."

"Tristan Dubrow." Tristan slips his laptop onto the table, stands, and they shake hands. Parker arrives a moment later.

After we've all greeted each other, and Parker and I exchange a couple of sentences about the Frick, Parker turns to Tristan. "Enough work. You're taking me back to the hotel. I'm tired and I want a soak in the bath."

Tristan snaps his laptop shut. "I got that number. Sent it by encrypted email."

"You got the number?" I ask. If it matches Bennett's, I'll know for certain that's how the hacker is getting in. A couple of hours with Tristan and I'm on the hacker's heels. "That's great," I say.

"I'll be in touch, Efa. We'll speak. Or message me on Telegram."

"I really appreciate it," I say.

"No worries."

Tristan and Parker leave Bennett and I on either side of the threshold to the flat, staring at each other. We stand in silence, our gazes locked, inches apart until the click of the elevator doors acts like some kind of "action" call in the movies.

"I'm sorry for being a jealous idiot," he says, and I can't help but soften at his confession.

"It's okay," I say. "I forgive you."

"But who was that?" he asks. "One of your thirty-nine brothers-in-law?"

I narrow my eyes at him like I'm not amused by his joke,

but it's funny. I head back over to my laptop. I want to make sure nothing's on display. Until I have unequivocal proof about what's going on, I'm not going to say anything to Bennett about my suspicions, and I don't want him finding out by accident.

"He's my sister-in-law's best friend's husband," I say, shutting down what I need to and locking my laptop.

He rolls his eyes, toes off his shoes, and pads over to the sofa. A sensation of relief settles in me. He's not come for a quick argument. He's planning to stay. A little while at least.

"All right," he says, encouraging me to elaborate. He sits close, pulls my feet over his legs and drags his knuckles down my cheek.

"He and Parker are in New York for the weekend and Eira put us in touch. He works in tech and thought it would be a good chance to meet and talk about options I have."

"Options?" he asks.

"Job options. Now I know I can't work at Fort. That one-night stand crushed my dreams."

He pulls me onto his lap. "Do you regret it?"

I sigh and sink into his chest. "How could I?"

"That's good to hear. I thought after this morning... things might have changed."

Our breathing begins to synchronize. As his chest rises and falls, my body moves with his. He's warm and safe and I don't ever want to fight with him. But... "Nothing's changed. I still... like you. And it's still frustrating as hell not being able to just *be*."

"But we *can* just be. I just met your brother-in-law's sister's uncle's niece."

I smile despite myself.

"We shook hands," he continues. "My name is actually Bennett Fordham. And that's who I introduced myself as."

"I know," I say. "But that's not all of who you are." I look up at him. "And all of who you are is pretty great. It would just be nice if I could be honest about that. But it doesn't matter. It's not like..."

I don't finish the end of my sentence.

It's not like this is a long-term thing.

It's not like I don't go back to London at the end of the summer.

It's not like you're going to change your mind. You've spent your entire adult life hiding.

He knows how this ends. I know how this ends. What's the point in making the time we have left miserable?

"It's not so difficult," he says. "I've lived like this a long time."

"Have you?" I stroke my finger along his jaw. "Like fully lived? You're hiding in hotel rooms, concerned about stalkers. Because why? I get you don't want to be famous. I get you don't want to bait the sycophants. But honestly, if you can't be who you are, on your own terms, how can you ever be free?"

He presses a kiss to my temple and we sit, entwined, able to hear each other's heartbeats in perfect tandem. For now.

He's not going to change. I get it. And I can talk to Eira, give her enough information so I don't feel bad and don't uncover Bennett at the same time. Because at the end of the summer, I'm going to walk away. I'd just rather not leave Bennett half the man he could be if things were different.

TWENTY-FIVE

Bennett

I roll to Efa's side, exhausted but still not sated. I never am with her. I don't know what it is about her, but I can't help but want more at every turn.

"You know how you said I could look into the security issues you're having?" she says from beside me.

"You came about fifteen seconds ago and now you're thinking about tech security. You really know how to kill the mood."

She laughs and cups my face in her hands. "What can I say?" she replies. "Maybe I'm just so overwhelmed that I have to distract myself with thoughts of tech."

"Okay, let's go with that theory." I gather her in my arms and pull her towards me, nuzzling into her neck. I don't know why, but this part—the time between the bouts of sex, when we're talking and feeling and just being—are becoming some of my favorite moments with Efa.

"Will you let me talk to your internal people so we can

compare notes? You didn't answer when I asked you before. And I know you think I couldn't possibly help, but what have you got to lose?"

"Notes about what?"

"About the attacks on your systems. Some patterns I noticed. Look, I know you've got the best in the business working for you and everything, but I've been doing some investigating and I think it might be worth pursuing."

"What have you found?" I ask, moving her legs so she's astride me.

She pushes up on my chest and sits, my hardening dick between her folds. "Nothing that stands up on its own, but I wonder if matching it up with your people's info might prove useful."

How can I say no to this woman? Do I think she's made some breakthrough about who's attacking Fort Inc. and why they seem to be closing in on us? No. Do I think it will do any harm? Also no.

"I can introduce you to Aarvi. She heads up my security team."

"Good," she says, rocking her hips back and forth in an absentminded way. The movement is more instinct than trying to start anything. She's getting comfortable. On my dick. And I don't hate it. "Can you call her?"

"Now?" I ask, grinning up at her. "With you naked, grinding against my cock?"

"Better now than in a couple of minutes when you'll be inside me," she says.

Fuck, Efa. How did I ever live without her sass?

I reach up and roll her nipple between my thumb and forefinger and she gasps, tipping her head back, thrusting herself against the sensation.

"Do it now, Bennett," she says. "Call her." She leans

forward, sliding herself up my dick, reaches for my phone on the nightstand, and tosses it onto my chest. "And be quick. I want to get laid."

That makes two of us.

I chuckle and dial Aarvi. It doesn't even ring once before she picks up.

"Hey, I want to put you in touch with someone I met who might have some information about the attacks. Efa Cadogan."

"Sure," she says. One of my favorite things about Aarvi is she doesn't use an unnecessary amount of words when she's talking to me. It means we can get to the meat of an issue quickly.

"You can be completely open with her." I grin up at Efa, who circles her hips in response. If I didn't know her better, I'd say she was using her body to get me to introduce her to Aarvi. But Efa's not manipulative. That's why she has such a problem not being more open with her sister. I get it. I really get it. I just can't do anything about it. I'm not going to let the last fifteen years' hard work keeping my identify as head of Fort Inc. a secret go to waste.

"Completely?" Aarvi asks.

I have to pause and steady my breathing as Efa grips my cock at the base, teasing the crown with her wet entrance. "Completely." I don't expect Efa to solve Fort's security issues. But she's not going to do any harm.

"Okay. Have her call me." I manage to keep my breathing steady as Efa watches me watching her.

"I'm sure she'll—" Efa slides down onto me and every part of me tenses. "She'll be in touch."

Efa nods, taking my free hand, and placing it back on her breast. I end the call and reach for a condom.

"Not yet," she says, her breathing ragged. "First, I want to come."

"Again?" I ask, teasingly.

"And again. And again. And again."

TWENTY-SIX

Efa

Of course I can't go to Fort's actual offices. No one other than employees are allowed through the doors. Lucky for me, they have a suite of meeting rooms in the same building where I *am* allowed to go.

The man at the reception desk gave me a pass card to Suite Three, similar to the ones at the hotel. He buzzes me through the double doors and I'm struck by how everything's entirely white. The floors, the walls, the carpet inset into the white marble tiles. I round the corner and find Suite Three. It's a small room with a white table and two white chairs. The entire place has the feel of a high-end insane asylum. I make a mental note to tease Bennett about it later.

The click-clack of heels draws my attention and the most gorgeous, glamorous woman on the planet opens the door. Her white linen suit is perfect camouflage in these meeting rooms. Her eyes are bright blue against her brown skin, and her hair looks so glossy I'm ninety percent certain she has a deal with L'Oreal.

"Aarvi?" I ask.

"Yes." Her wide mouth pulls into a huge grin. "You must be Efa. I'm excited to meet you."

"I'm not sure you're going to remain excited," I say as I take a seat. "I'm sure you know much more about all this than me, but I wanted to show you what I found, in case it's helpful."

"I appreciate it," she says. She doesn't give away that this meeting is probably a pain in her arse and the last thing she wants to be doing today.

"Shall I take you through what I know?"

"That would be great," she says, her smile never faltering, not even for a second.

I flip open my laptop and go through what I've learned, including how the attacks happen in a weekly pattern and how Tristan discovered the attacks seem to be routed through Bennett's phone. Her expression remains neutral throughout.

"So that's it really," I say, sitting back in my white chair. "I'm not sure if any of it's useful."

She pulls in a breath and her gaze flits between me and my laptop screen. "Yes," she says, but I'm not quite sure what that means. "I've been aware of much of this for a few days now. Ten days, I think." She sighs.

So she knows the attacks are coming through Bennett's phone? How is it possible that *he* doesn't seem to know that? "Ten days?" I ask, when the real question I want to ask is why she hasn't told Bennett that his phone is putting Fort Inc. at risk.

"Yeah. I've been trying to... I don't know how well you know Bennett, but he doesn't trust a lot of people."

"I know that much," I say.

She nods. "I guessed you would when he asked me to meet with you. He wouldn't have done that if he didn't trust you."

"I think he does," I say.

"Can I ask why you haven't told him what you've found?" she asks. It's the exact question I want to ask her.

"Because I don't..." I let the sentence taper off, then start again. "Someone has to be physically close to his phone to be able to get and renew their access, since the firewalls are changed and renewed every twenty-four hours. Just because you got access one time, unless you penetrate the systems on the first attempt, you need ongoing access—"

"Right," she says—and of course I'm explaining something she already knows.

"So that means whoever's attacking Fort Inc. has regular access to Ben."

"Right," she says again.

Silence settles between us. Neither of us says what we're both thinking.

"He doesn't trust a lot of people," she says again, finally.

"And it will break him to know that someone he *does* trust has betrayed him," I reply. "I was looking for something conclusive."

"I'd like to map his movements," she says. "When he's at the hotel, that's easy. I don't think it's coming from there. He's not going to let his phone out of his sight when there are strangers in his room. Apart from that, do you know of any regular meetings he has where he'd leave his phone unattended? I've gotten details on his personal trainer, who checks out. It's definitely not him. I've obviously checked everyone at Fort. He doesn't have a driver..."

I nod, understanding that she will have ruled out all the

obvious suspects. That's not where my suspicions lie. I just don't know if she knows about Bennett's Monday night gathering.

"Is there anyone else you can think of?" Aarvi asks.

"Yeah," I say. "There is."

TWENTY-SEVEN

Efa

The lobby of Leo's building looks like a futuristic science lab. Everything is bright white marble and glass—a blank slate. It's the exact opposite of what I need right now, which is distraction. I'm trying to think of something other than the burner phone in my pocket and whether or not one of Bennett's best friends is betraying him. I want resolution for Bennett. I just don't want the resolution I suspect we're going to get.

"I need my shades," Bennett says, nudging me as we stand hand in hand, waiting for the woman behind the desk to call up to Leo.

I'm zoned out and he knows it. I turn my face up to him, giving him my full attention, which is what he deserves. I can't help but smile. "I thought you'd like it. Your meeting rooms look very much like this."

"Do they?" he asks, his brow furrowed.

My smile widens. "Have you never been?"

"Not for a while. I don't remember what they look like."

I laugh and feel it in my belly. Bennett's one of the cleverest men on the planet, but some things don't even register in that brain of his. It's adorable.

Then my smile fades. Maybe his best friend's betrayal isn't registering with him either. He's a smart man. Why hasn't he investigated those closest to him?

Because he trusts them.

It's like someone's got their stiletto on my toe. It hurts, because if what Aarvi and I suspect is true, Bennett's going to be hurting.

"Go ahead, sir, madam," the woman behind the desk says as she puts down the phone. "It's the penthouse."

"Of course it is." I roll my eyes and we head toward the lifts. "Do you think you'll ever be friends with someone who doesn't have money?"

"None of my friends had money before business school. Oh, apart from Worth. And Jack of course. He's American royalty." He holds the lift doors open and ushers me inside.

"So you had to make the others rich so they were acceptable to you?"

"Yes, Efa, everyone around me has to have at least ten million in the bank or I can't even look at them."

Why do I find such a dry sense of humor so completely sexy?

I laugh. "It's not fun if you don't bite."

He raises his eyebrows and presses a kiss to the top of my head. "Thanks for coming tonight," he says.

"Wouldn't miss it." It's true on lots of different levels.

Bennett asking me to Monday night sports again is a complete win. When I left the meeting with Aarvi, I wasn't sure how I was going to engineer an invite—I just knew there was no other way. I'd been musing on ideas, everything from saying I had the urge to make a lamb curry and we should invite his friends to watch Monday night sports at my place, to calling up Nadia and asking her if she was planning on attending, so I could tell Bennett and offer to accompany him again to keep her occupied. Not that it worked last time. I even thought about suggesting I could arrange mani-pedis for us to keep Nadia from licking Leo's ear for an hour.

In the end, I didn't have to think of any elaborate schemes, because Bennett just assumed I was coming. Like, where else would I be but by his side?

"Do you normally take it in turns between each other's places?" I ask.

"Normally we'll go to a restaurant or a bar. Sometimes a private members club—depending on what's going on with everyone and how private we need to be. But at the moment, because of what's happening at Fort, we're keeping our meetings even more low-key."

"So Monday night sports isn't much about sport?"

"We always make sure there's a screen somewhere around. But as you could probably tell when we were at Worth's place, it's not central to our evening."

"Do you think Nadia's a permanent member of your Monday Night Club?"

Bennett groans. "I hope not. As long as they don't announce their engagement."

"Yes, because we haven't brought any champagne. Or a gift. Or anything." I try to look mock panicked, and it has the intended effect. Bennett laughs. "Don't worry, he'll still love you if he gets married, Bennett."

He narrows his eyes at me and takes my hand. The lift doors open on the penthouse floor and we fall silent.

Before we can knock, Leo answers the door. "My favorite people. Come in."

Leo strikes me as a guy who's happy for at least three hundred and sixty-three days of the year. But he's positively effervescent tonight, and a small part of me thinks it might be because he *did* actually get engaged.

"We're celebrating!" Leo says.

My stomach slips sideways and I squeeze Bennett's hand. This seriously can't be happening, can it?

"We just got through some really important permits at the New River development." He slaps Bennett on the back and presses a kiss against my cheek. "Come on, guys. Let's do some tequila."

This is good news. It's not an engagement.

Worth and Bennett exchange a look as we get into Leo's main living area. It's a huge space with three separate areas of seating and windows across two walls, framing views of the Manhattan skyline.

Nadia sees me, throws up her hands and rushes toward me like we're long-lost friends.

Except we're not. We didn't even connect particularly well last time we met.

"Have some tequila." She grabs two shot glasses and presses them into my and Bennett's hands.

"Congratulations," I say, trying to smile enough for Bennett and me, because I know Bennett won't be doing his share.

"More!" Nadia says, picking up the bottle and offering out the tequila. "Let's party."

I don't need to be holding Bennett's hand to know how awkward he feels. I know he doesn't like Nadia, but she's Leo's choice. He's going to have to learn to get on with her. It will be better when we can figure out who's attacking Fort and Monday nights can go back to being public gatherings. Or as public as a gathering in a private club can be. Then maybe Nadia won't get invited and Bennett can get his friend back once a week at least.

Someone flips on the TV and the guys all settle on couches.

"I'm going to put out some snacks," Nadia says.

"I'll help if you like," I say.

She shoots me a smile. "No worries, I got it. I quite like playing house." She starts bustling around in a way that tacitly communicates she knows the kitchen well. I settle on a barstool as she pulls out bowls and plates, putting together some dips and crudites as well as crisps and other snacks I can't identify.

She darts between the kitchen and the living area, ferrying food and drinks. She's like a fifties housewife in training.

"Okay, so I'm going to freshen up. Are you okay here?" she asks. It's nice of her to check. And she's obviously more comfortable having some distance between her and Leo tonight. Maybe because she's on home territory. She feels a bit more secure. I hope so. Bennett might warm to her if she gives him a bit of room.

"Of course. I need to check my emails." I pull out my phone.

She groans. "My inbox is out of control," she says. "I think I need to hire someone. Back in a minute. Or ten."

She leaves, and I pull out my phone. When Aarvi and I both admitted that we were reluctant to tell Bennett it was *his* phone acting as a gateway into Fort, Aarvi opened up about some of her other findings. She's convinced the reason the attacker can't be pinpointed is because the malware isn't attaching to Bennett's phone. It only routes through his phone, which means the attacker needs to act while Bennett's phone is nearby.

I wander over to the sofas and pretend to be interested in whatever's on the TV, while checking out who's sitting where and what phones are on display. Bennett has his phone on the table in front of him, between his legs and a bowl of corn chips. There are two phones nearby. I assume one is Worth's and one is Leo's, since they're sitting either side of Bennett on the couch. But it's not a sure thing. The malware could be coming from any of the four phones near Bennett's right now. Aarvi said they'd have to be within a meter radius, and that means all of them are probably in range, but probably isn't going to cut it. I need certainty. I'm not sure I'll have an opportunity like this again.

I back off, returning to the kitchen stools. As subtly as I can, I bend to check under the couch for any additional phones hiding underneath the sofas. Maybe one's been planted.

At that moment, Leo stands and I bolt upright, in case he thinks it's weird I'm peering under his sofa. "Shit, I'm sorry."

I glance at the table and realize he's knocked over a bottle of beer.

"I'll get a towel."

I run to the kitchen, pull some paper towel from the counter and race back. Leo takes it from me and mops up the table. Bennett tears off some towel and dries his phone before slipping it into his back pocket.

Perfect. Now there's no doubt he's in range if I drop the phone Aarvi gave me down the back of the sofa.

The phone Aarvi gave me is the exact make and model as my own. This additional phone should be able to track any malware being sent to Bennett's phone.

I'd never make a spy. I'm just not cut out for lying and deceit. My pulse races as I stuff my real phone into my blazer pocket and pull out the second phone from my jeans. It's either now or never. I have to put this phone near Bennett before Nadia comes back or I might not get another chance to go unnoticed.

I grab the tequila bottle from the counter and stalk over to the sofas. "You want this?" I ask, holding the bottle over the back of the sofa.

Bennett grabs it. "Thanks." He slides it onto the table in front of me and I push my fingers into the short hair above his neck. Then I place a kiss on his head while slipping the phone behind the cushion he's leaning on.

No one seems to notice and I back away, mentally high-fiving myself. I grab my phone and tap out a text to Aarvi, telling her the phone's in place. She's on standby, ready to do whatever she needs to do to trace the malware back to the attacker's phone. As much as it will devastate Bennett if we discover the source of the hacks is one of his most trusted friends, the alternative is worse. I want to protect him from people who are going to hurt him, and that means, tonight, we need answers.

MONDAY NIGHT SEEMS to last at least three and a half days, and I'm hoping that means Aarvi has the time she needs to do her job.

On the upside, Nadia has been more than charming. She's sat in her own chair for almost the whole evening, and has even refrained from licking Leo's ear. I'm sure Bennett will be more inclined to like her given we've been chatting for the last three hours in between Nadia's frequent trips to the bathroom. She's either got a drug problem or a UTI.

"These games go on forever, don't they?" I say to her.

"Why can't they stick to proper football like the rest of the world?" she asks.

I laugh, even though I'm not sure she's joking. "I was thinking the same thing."

Bennett looks over his shoulder and our eyes lock. The game is over from what I can tell. The score looks like one side beat the other side to death. "We need to go," he says, his eyes not leaving mine.

Since I messaged Aarvi, I haven't dared pull out my phone again to see if she's messaged back with news. I didn't want there to be any chance that Nadia saw me with two phones. Although the boys have been distracted, there's always a chance one of them is paying closer attention than I realize.

I haven't wanted to take any unnecessary risks. I can only hope I've done enough and Aarvi has been able to figure out the attacker.

As everyone stands, still continuing their conversations, I slide off the barstool. I just want to get out of here as soon as possible. At the same time, I want to pause time. If Aarvi has found the source of the attacks, I'm going to have to have a very difficult conversation with Bennett.

Casually, I pat my jeans pockets and glance around. "Have you seen my phone?" I ask Nadia.

She shakes her head. I deliberately didn't bring a bag with me today. I didn't want to draw any attention to myself.

"Bennett, do you have my phone?"

He frowns at me and shakes his head. He's probably wondering why I'm asking him. There's no reason why he'd have my phone.

I clap my hands on my jeans pockets and head to the sofa. I glance around the area like I don't know exactly where I've left the phone. I pull at the cushions, checking behind and then, like magic, find what I'm looking for. "Phew," I say to myself, loud enough that I hope it sounds convincing to anyone who's listening.

I turn to find Bennett staring right at me, his expression thunderous.

We say our goodbyes. Worth leaves at the same time and Bennett doesn't say a word to either of us as we ride the lift down to the lobby. He doesn't even hold my hand. He grips me by my elbow, like he thinks I'm about to run somewhere.

"Catch you later," I say to Worth. I don't get a chance to give him a kiss goodbye before Bennett leads me forcefully out of the building and onto the street.

"Hey," I say, pulling away from him. "What are you doing?"

"What am I doing?" he spits. "What are *you* doing?"

"What?" I ask, but he doesn't answer and we get into his car in silence.

"Why are you so angry?" I ask again as he starts the engine.

"Why did you drop your phone behind the cushion where I was sitting?"

I sigh. I really hope we don't go to war and assign me to the intelligence division. I'm a terrible spy. How did he possibly catch that?

"I'm waiting for an explanation," he says, and I can hear real venom in his words. It's not a tone I've ever heard from him. He's usually so calm and collected.

I fix my stare straight ahead through the windscreen. I can't bear to see him so angry. "It was a phone Aarvi gave me."

"Aarvi?" he asks. "What? Why?"

There's no getting out of the corner I've painted myself into. There's nothing I can do other than tell him the truth.

"You know Tristan, my not-brother-in-law?"

"The guy in your apartment."

"I'll state again for the record that he's very happily married. But I didn't tell you the entire truth about him."

He pulls out into the street and he heads in the direction of my place.

"I'm waiting," he says.

"He's in tech. I didn't lie about that. And it's kinda true that he's been helping me think about my career. But that's not why I met up with him. I wanted his help in tracking down the person or organization responsible for the Fort security breaches."

"You told him?"

I let out a breath. "I did." I turn to him in my seat, hoping he'll see that I'm telling the truth. "But he's, like, the best in the business. And a family friend. He's not going to do anything that's—"

"And?" His jaw is so tight, it might shatter at any moment.

"And he helped me with a theory I had about where the attacks are coming from."

"What theory?"

"Well... then I met Aarvi."

"What theory, Efa?"

I ignore his question, because I'm getting to it and I don't want to be rushed. "Turns out, Aarvi had a similar theory. So we worked together to test it out."

"Tonight?" he asks.

"Yes," I say.

We pull up in front of my building and I go to get out,

but before I do, he locks the car doors. "I want to hear your theory."

I'm irritated that he's locked us in, but this is Bennett Fordham. He's used to getting what he wants.

"Aarvi and I both think—and in fact, Aarvi has proof, and Tristan also discovered—that it was your phone that gave the attacker a gateway into the Fort systems."

His eyes narrow slightly but he faces forward, not looking at me as I speak.

"But to be able to do that," I continue, "Aarvi explained that someone would have to be close by to you, because the malware isn't sitting on your device. The attacker is smart and doesn't want to give away how they're getting in. So the malware only *routes* through your phone. I've never even heard of that. Aarvi said they'd have to put a mobile device within a meter of your phone to gain access."

He lets out a hardened half-laugh. "So you slipped a phone down the back of a cushion so you could route malware through my phone, then had the backup of five other people in the room as a cover. Did you do this on your own or are you and Tristan working together?"

"What?" I snap. "Stop being an asshole for a second. I'm trying everything I can to help you. You can't think I'm responsible for the attacks."

"I don't know about *entirely* responsible. But it sounds like maybe you're part of it. Why else would you put on a show—a *bad* show, I might add—about your phone being lost in the couch?"

"Because, dickwad, Aarvi has control over that device and she's trying to pick up the attack in real time." I try the door handle again and it's still locked. "Let me out of here. I'm trying to help you and you accuse me? You're a real distrusting piece of shit. I've never given you the slightest reason not to trust me."

"And neither have the five men up there who you're accusing of sabotaging me."

"Yeah, you're right. That's who I think is attacking Fort. One of them. One of your best friends. And it's horrible and it makes me feel sick that someone could do that to you, but it's definitely not me doing it."

"There's no way."

Of course he doesn't believe me. "If you don't want to hear it from me, then maybe you'll listen to Aarvi."

I pull out my phone to see if she's sent me any news, but there's nothing. She said she'd message as soon as she knew anything.

"Let me out," I say.

"I'm going to call her," he says, not opening the door.

"Call her. But let me out. I'll be waiting for your apology."

He unlocks the car doors, his phone already pressed to his ear.

I'd really like to know what Aarvi says. But at the same time, I'm done. I don't want to be the person Bennett immediately looks to if something goes wrong. I slam the car door shut and head into my building.

I'm exhausted.

I want to be at home.

I want my sister.

I want a KitKat and an episode of *Love Island*.

I understand Bennett has trust issues, but I'm not sure I can handle being the prime suspect the moment something goes wrong. I've worked my arse off trying to get some kind of resolution for him. Then for him to turn around and suspect me? After all the time we've spent together? I understand people used his mother. But he's not her, and I'm not them.

The lift doors are closing and I'm half waiting to see if Bennett appears before they do, his expression full of apology. Again.

But he doesn't.

And after an hour of waiting for him to pound on my door, I turn off the light and try to sleep.

TWENTY-EIGHT

Bennett

She should have told me, but I understand why she didn't. I tip my head back on my headrest and sigh.

"And you know this for certain?"

"Do you recognize the number?" she asks. "That's definitely the cell that's been facilitating the attacks."

"I don't understand why Leo would use his own number. Wouldn't it be easier just to buy a burner and use that?"

"I can't answer that," Aarvi says. "But it's definitely coming through that cell. I have no doubt about that. Always this time of night, early in the week. Everything tracks."

"And Efa helped?"

"Without her, I would have had to come to you with my suspicions and you would have shut me down and we'd be making no progress whatsoever."

"I wouldn't have shut you down," I snap.

"Bennett, you're very loyal to your friends. There's no

way you would have entertained the idea that one of them had betrayed you."

I don't respond. I'm so careful with people I don't know. So distant. But with my five best friends? I'm as open with them as I am with anyone.

"Is it possible that someone could be covering their tracks by using Leo's phone?" I ask.

Aarvi doesn't respond right away.

"Even if there's a zero point one percent chance, I want to verify these findings," I say.

"There's a chance," she says. "They could be routing it through Leo's phone as a cover. It's unlikely."

"But possible."

"Yes." I can tell she believes it's Leo, but she doesn't know him like I do. "There are lots of reasons why he might be doing this. He could have run into money difficulties."

"Leo's got plenty of money."

"But maybe he's a gambler or has made some bad decisions. It could be sport for all we know. Plenty of attacks are just for the fun of it. But—"

"You're right." I cut her off. "Let's do some checks."

"On Leo?"

"On everyone." My friends are my safe zone. The people I can go to to let off steam about work or bounce ideas off. To them, I could admit when I wasn't getting the results I wanted from my business or my life or whatever other area might be falling short of expectations.

But those five people don't feel safe anymore.

Nothing does.

Aarvi's right. I wouldn't have believed her if she'd told me someone in my inner circle was responsible for the attacks. That would have been a mistake.

"Make sure you include Efa in those checks," I say.

"Efa? That doesn't make sense. She's been trying to help."

"Maybe," I reply.

Maybe she's been trying to push blame onto others. There's no doubt these attacks started to worsen just before she blew into town.

"What do I need to know about her?"

"I've already had a security check done. Everything seemed okay, but I want her rechecked."

"I'll arrange that, but for what it's worth, I don't think she's anything to worry about."

"I like to deal with data rather than guesswork."

"She's never pushed me for any information at all. In all my dealings with her, there's been nothing to make me suspect she might be part of the attacks."

"Just check her out." I don't want to continue rehashing things. I'll do that in the privacy of my hotel room tonight. "So next Monday, do we run the checks again? I can take the tracking device. That way, I know it hasn't been tampered with."

"We can certainly double-check."

I don't feel safe with my friends now, but I'm not going after any of them until I have definitive proof. "We need to be as sure as we are that water is wet. And then we need to triple-check."

I haven't told Aarvi about Tristan. But something about that situation didn't sit well with me.

"Ever heard of Tristan Dubrow?" I ask.

"The hacker?" Aarvi asks. "Of course. He's a legend."

"Apparently Efa enlisted his help."

"Wow. He doesn't come cheap. How did she even know how to get in contact with him? It's not like he's got an enquiry form on his website."

"A friend of the family, apparently."

"That's a big favor to call in."

I push out a breath. So far, what Efa has said is consistent with what Aarvi's saying. Maybe Efa's concocting some elaborate hoax, but my gut says she's told me the truth.

It doesn't mean my anger with her has waned. It hasn't. She should have told me what she was doing. I expect honesty from the people I'm close with. And especially from her.

She understands why people being who they say they are is so important to me. And still she went behind my back. God only knows how long she's had this theory about one of my inner circle betraying me. Why wouldn't she come to me? Why wouldn't she say? I'm mad Aarvi didn't tell me, but that's a professional disappointment. Efa not saying anything cuts deeper.

"You're convinced he's one of the good guys?" I ask.

"Who really knows, but his reputation is for saving the day. He's like a hacker superhero. They say he's prevented Russia from doing all sort of nefarious things to western governments."

I roll my eyes. A hacker superhero? "Why have I never heard of him?"

Aarvi laughs. "Coming from you? The ultimate hidden man? Anyway, it's different. Hackers don't want people knowing their identity."

"Set things up for Monday. Then we'll see where we are."

"I'll get the security checks run and set everything up for Monday..." She's got something else she wants to say. I hate it when my team don't speak freely. That's what got us into this mess in the first place. I need people around me who don't treat me as the boss. As the billionaire. That's part of what had attracted me to Efa—she didn't give a shit about my wealth or status. But she had a different agenda.

"What, Aarvi?" I snap. "You have to tell me everything."

"I was just going to say that I'd happily stake money on the fact that Efa is on our side."

I can't think about that now. I just want to focus on catching whoever it is that's attacking Fort.

I need to *know*, not just *believe*, who I can trust.

TWENTY-NINE

Efa

As I take the staff lift to the Park Suite, I can't help but wonder if any of the other housekeeping staff has a side gig? I've been trying to track down a hacker going after one of the most successful companies in American corporate history. Maybe Jose and Jackie, who work the executive rooms, have a sideline dealing shares in corporate bonds.

My stomach flips as the lift stops at my floor and the doors slide open. My heart lunges heavily when the door to the Park Suite comes into view.

I'm on my own today. Marcella is sick and I've been given sole responsibility for her rooms. She's taught me well —I know I can do it. I just wish I didn't have to. Not today. I don't want to see Bennett in these circumstances.

Even though I last saw him a few hours ago, I miss him. But it's not because of the time that's passed, it's because of the distance now stretched between us. Even though we fought and he overreacted, the idea of him not wanting to see me makes my heart ache.

He's not reached out since we talked in the car yesterday. Aarvi can't have convinced him that it's not me who's out to get him.

All I've been doing is trying to help.

He doesn't trust people, I get it, but it hurts more than it should that he doesn't trust *me*.

The last thing I want to do is change his sheets when he might think I'm there to spy on him or plant some kind of device to aid in the attack on Fort. I don't want to see him again when he sees me as the enemy, because that's the last thing I am. I can't bear to see an expression of hatred or distrust in his eyes. Not after everything we've shared.

The light to make up the room is on. I arrange the trolley outside, pull my shoulders back, and knock on the door. I open the door with a second knock and call "housekeeping". There's no answer, but I wouldn't expect Bennett to answer.

Trying to put off seeing him, I head to the bathroom first. I collect all the used towels and head back out into the corridor to stuff them in my linen sack. For a moment, I can breathe. Not for long. I head back to the bathroom with my cleaning bucket and start on the sink.

Something's off. I can't put my finger on it. And then I realize. His toiletries have gone.

I spin around, trying to spot them somewhere, but there's nothing. Not even his brown leather washbag. I back out of the bathroom and head to the dressing room, pulling the doors open.

Nothing.

No suit jackets. No shirts. No shoes.

It's all gone.

I run into the bedroom. Bennett never left personal items in the room, but I search for something, anything—a phone charger, a computer mouse. But there's no doubt about it: he's checked out.

Where's he gone?

Somewhere he can hide from me. My heart feels so heavy, I can barely breathe from the weight of it.

That's it. No discussion. No goodbye. We're just done.

I go through the motions in a daze, all the while replaying our last conversation with tiny variations—things I could have said, maybe should have said, that might have resulted in a different outcome. But for all my mental gymnastics, I don't see how things *wouldn't* have ended just like this. We started as we began, with Bennett thinking I'm something I'm not.

After the bathroom, I move through the suite, trying not to imagine him sitting on the sofa or at the desk. In the bed.

As I pull off the pillowcases, his scent fills my lungs. It all feels so unfair. I'm angry that he couldn't just talk it out with me. Why couldn't he see that I was trying to protect him? It must be awful to know there are so few people in the world you can trust, and then have one of the few in your inner sanctum betray you.

I get it. I've been there. But why couldn't he let me be there for him?

After making the bed, I start dusting, wiping any sign of Bennett from every surface.

That's when I see it. The stone I wrangled from Bennett's hand that day at the lake. The one I asked him to keep safe.

He left it.

My knees weaken and I take a seat on the bed, even though I've just made it, because I'll fall to the floor if I don't. The stone feels smooth in my hand, and warm like it's been in the sun all day.

He must have known I'd find it.

He wanted to rid himself of every last memory of me, like I'm some kind of disease to be purged from his system.

I guess I should be grateful for the closure.

I can go back to London in a few weeks with no loose ends or regrets. There's nothing to wonder "what if" about.

Even though I didn't expect things to end this way, they were always going to end. We were never going to ride off into the sunset together. And that's why I can't understand why it feels like my body is shutting down. My chest aches and my legs aren't strong enough to hold me.

How can I feel so much for someone who trusts me so little?

It hurts at the moment, but hopefully it will pass quickly.

It doesn't stop me slipping the stone into my pocket.

He might not want to relive the memories of our time together, but if memories are all we have, I'll take every last one.

THIRTY

Bennett

Monday night has always been the social highlight of the week. I'm not anyone but myself on those evenings.

Not a boss.

Not a billionaire.

Not a movie star's son.

Tonight feels very different, in no small part because I'm carrying two devices that are essentially going to spy on my friends. It doesn't feel good. The idea that at the end of this evening, I'll know for certain whether one of them is trying to attack me, feels worse.

We're back at Worth's place tonight. The venue was discussed on the group chat, but I'm not sure why we ended up here. I just skipped to the end.

There's one bright spot in the evening—Nadia's not going to be here. That piece of information caught my attention on the chat.

Surprisingly, Leo answers the door, and I take a step down in shock.

I hadn't put my game face on.

"Wow, you look pissed," Leo says. "What's the matter?"

I shrug. "Tired. What's your excuse for looking like *that*?" I ask as I push past him.

Leo chuckles. He's always in a good mood. Is it all an act? Does he hate me? If he needed money, why didn't he just ask? Any of the five of us would have done anything for him.

I'm trying to keep an open mind, but I've seen the data. I made Aarvi take me through it this week and the evidence against Leo is compelling. I just want to see it all for myself.

I'm still holding on to some threads of hope. Efa could be lying—it could all have been an elaborate misdirection to protect her or whoever she's working for.

Every time I think of her, it's like slicing open a fresh wound. I just want to put a bandage on and forget about her.

Heal.

I've got to push past it and get through tonight.

Aarvi and I went through the devices that could track the attacks. We've got the same thing that Efa used, and then something bigger with quicker processing power that's the size of a tablet. I've had it sewn into my jacket and I'll keep it nearby.

I'm the first to arrive after Leo. Worth hands me a glass of whisky with an oversized ice cube, like he's been expecting me.

"Cheers," he says, holding up his own glass.

Leo knocks my glass with his beer bottle and we head to the sofa.

As if it's uncomfortable, I take my cell from my pants pocket and slide it onto the table in front of us. Except it's not uncomfortable and it's not my cell. It's the tracker.

I'm sure she's fine in different circumstances, but having someone else here on a Monday night, among the six of us, alters the dynamic.

The dynamic.

Can our easy friendship really have been faked for all these years? And if it started off real, when did it go sour? How long has Leo been pretending? And is it personal to me or does he hate us all? Was I a planned target or just in the wrong place at the wrong time?

"You okay?" Worth asks, pulling my attention from my own thoughts.

"Yeah," I reply.

"How's Efa?" he asks.

I glance across at Leo, who's wrestling with the remote control. I turn my attention back to Worth and shrug.

"Had a fight?"

I nod. "She's young," I say. I don't want to get into it.

"She didn't seem that way to me," Worth says. "But I haven't spent much time with her."

She doesn't seem that way to me, either. I don't know if it's because her parents died when she was so young or that she's had to put up with so much since, but she was older than her years. Apart from that first night together, I never really noticed the age gap between us.

But was that part of the plan? Maybe she just tried to be everything I might have wanted in order to get close to me.

I rub the bridge of my nose. My mind's still so full of her. I can't keep a lid on my thoughts. The more I try to push her away, the more vivid my memories.

"How's work?" I ask Worth. When he doesn't answer, I glance over at him.

He looks between Leo and me. "Good."

"Good," I say.

Is it me making this awkward, or is it Worth? Is he in on it? Does he know what Leo is doing? Are they all trying to bring me down?

"I'm going for a shit," I say. I need some time to recalibrate. If I carry on like this, I'll give the game away.

"Thanks for telling us," Leo says. "Do you need one of us to help or something?"

"Fuck off," I say, and it feels like the first honest thing I've said since I got here. If Aarvi and Efa turn out to be right, I will ruin Leo.

There will be nothing anyone can do to stop me from bringing him to his knees in every way imaginable. He will end up rotting in a southeast Asian prison, penniless, his reputation ruined.

But I need proof first.

I leave my phone on the table. As I stand, I wonder if I should take my jacket with me. If someone picks it up, it'll be clear that I'm carrying something in there. But if I take my jacket to the bathroom, I'm sure to get shit for it.

In the end, I abandon it and head out. Hopefully by the time I get back, Jack, Fisher, and Byron will have arrived, and Worth's spotlight will be off me.

I head back into the living room exactly seven minutes later. I figure that's an acceptable time to have a shit, not that I've ever timed myself.

I haven't brought my actual cell with me. I didn't want to risk having too many devices on me, but I can't help wondering whether Aarvi has gotten the data she needs by now. I want to get out of here as soon as possible. But ESPN hasn't even been turned on yet.

I've got hours of this torture left. I have to sit here, wondering who's my friend and who's my enemy. Did my mother feel this way all the time? Did she constantly wonder who was using her and who genuinely wanted to spend time in her company—not because she was rich or famous, just because they liked *her*?

I don't allow myself to miss her. Not anymore. Her loss drove me on for the first few years after her death—my need for survival fueling my business decisions, helping build my fortune. But every now and then, I'd like to be sure of someone. Anyone.

I thought I had that in my friends, and now even that's gone to shit.

What am I left with?

I manage to sit through the next three hours without flinching every time Leo speaks to me. But it's not easy. And now I can't help questioning everything Worth says or does, as well.

Why are we at his place again? Are he and Leo making sure these evenings happen at one of their places to ensure things go according to some secret plan? Is that how I ended up here? Was I tricked? I wish I had my phone so I could scroll through my messages. Why didn't Fisher, Jack, or Byron offer to host?

Maybe they're in on it too.

I scrub my hand through my hair as if I'm trying to pull every thought from my brain.

"You seem really focused on the game tonight, Bennett," Fisher says.

It's almost like I've forgotten people can see me. I'm losing it.

"What can I say? I'm a Broncos fan," I deadpan. I get up to go and fix myself a drink. "Anyone want anything?" I ask.

"Sure, I'll take another beer," Leo says.

Next Monday if he asks me for a drink, I might be

lacing it with arsenic. I head over to the bar and it feels good to get some space.

Until Worth follows me. He doesn't say anything, just takes the bottle from me and tops up his whisky. He grabs more ice from the machine and plops a huge cube into my drink, then another into his.

"You know you could talk to her," he says. "I've never seen you with anyone who seems to get you. And isn't equal parts intimidated and hoping to get a ring on her finger."

My brain careens from thoughts of my friend's betrayal to thoughts of Efa. What's worse? Her betrayal or Leo's?

"Yeah, she wasn't intimidated," I think aloud. "That would have been..." Worth's right, if she was trying to get close to me to launch an attack on Fort Inc., she would have been more likely to have been submissive and uber charming rather than call me, what was it? Oh yes, dickwad.

I really hope it's not her.

But that means it's Leo. I'm not sure what hurts worse.

"Is it irreparable?" he asks.

I sigh. I haven't spoken to her in a week. I have no idea if she's even still in the country. "I don't know."

Finally, I reach my limit. I need to be alone. "I'm out." I can't bear pretending to be anyone but myself among these five people. And I won't do it any longer.

I grab my phone and jacket and head out—ready to find out who has betrayed me.

THIRTY-ONE

Bennett

I'm used to being called cold and emotionless. It doesn't bother me. It's not that I don't feel anything, I'm just used to doing the feeling inside. I don't like to show people what's going on.

"Your pacing is making me nervous," Aarvi says.

I understand her nerves. She's not used to seeing me like this any more than I'm used to being like this.

"So it's definitely Leo?" I ask.

She told me last night, but I wanted her to go through everything again today.

"Definitely." She winces slightly, but I catch it.

"What?"

"There's just one thing that doesn't add up."

"Tell me," I say.

"Well, yesterday, I replicated some of our systems—put dummy files in and routed the hack through there."

"So they *think* they got into Fort but didn't?"

She nods. "Yes. I was hoping it might lead to some kind

of clue as to what they're looking for. The only thing is... I don't know, maybe I'm misreading it, but it's like they knew it was a booby trap. The door was open but they didn't come through."

Efa's face comes to mind. "Efa knew we were on the case. She'd probably guess that we'd rerun the trace."

She shakes her head. "This isn't Efa. She and I chatted and it's clear she's out of her depth with this. She relied on Tristan heavily. She's been taught the right stuff by professors, but she hasn't had experience putting it into practice."

"How can you be sure?"

"Some of the questions she's asking. The assumptions she's making. This is routing through Leo's phone. But I wonder if there's someone using that as a cover."

"I suggested that. But who?" I ask.

"It didn't seem probable before, especially as the only people to have access to you were the five guys plus Efa—"

And then the penny drops like a fucking ton of bricks on my foot. "Nadia."

"Who?" Aarvi asks.

"Leo's girlfriend. New girlfriend. Fuck. Fuck. Fuck! She's been right there in front of me. Why didn't I think about her?"

"Who is she?"

"She's appeared out of nowhere." I let out an ironic laugh. "Fuck, she's been submissive and uber charming. Can't leave him alone for five seconds. Christ, it's not Efa, it's Nadia. Get Chul on the phone. We need him to check her out immediately."

Chul tells us it's going to take some time to check out Nadia. After all, I have no surname or photo, and a quick search reveals she has zero social media presence. Maybe Efa would have more details about her—she sacrificed more than one night trying to run interference for me—but that situation is complicated. Until I can get certainty on Nadia, I'm not speaking to anyone about this situation.

I need to be sure. About everyone and everything.

But relief floods through me like a collapsed damn. I don't know what I'd have left if Leo had been the one betraying me. Or any of my friends. I'm not sure I could have handled it. And now I don't have to.

"Thank fucking god," I say out loud, because I can't keep it in any longer.

It's not Leo.

It's not Efa.

I feel it in my gut. Yes, I want confirmation. I want to understand who and why and every other detail. But at the same time, the hurricane inside me has slowed to a breeze.

If it's not my friends, and it's not Efa. This will be rough for Leo, but he's strong and he'll get through it. At least it's no one any of us have known for long—not someone part of our inner circle.

THIRTY-TWO

Efa

Having so many shifts at the hotel over the past week has been a blessing in disguise. It's helped camouflage the hurt I've been feeling, pushed it under the rug with a quick shove. But now, on my day off, I'm exhausted from the pretense. And I'm aware of the hurt in every part of my heart.

I feel so abandoned by Bennett. He was so quick to believe the worst in me and it was so easy for him to walk away. Maybe my feelings for him weren't reciprocated, but I thought... What did I think? I must have misread so much, misunderstood the connection I thought we had.

"I'm worried about you," Eira says as I balance the phone on the pillow beside me so I don't have to use energy holding it. "You look pale."

"I haven't seen sunlight in eight days." It's a slight exaggeration, but not much of one. I've been at work for seven in the morning and home at six at night. I'm tired. And I'm kinda heartbroken.

"When do you come home back to London?" she asks. "Does Gretal need you that much? You were meant to have a flexible arrangement. Can't she flexibly let you come back home?"

Should I go back to London? Realistically, I'm sure I could find a reason to go back that Gretal would understand. I was only meant to be here another couple of weeks anyway.

There are so many things to miss about home: the buzz I feel walking through Covent Garden, the way my sister is just a few minutes away, the way there's a place for everyone, no matter who you are.

"I'm homesick," I confess.

"Come back," she says.

There's only one thing in New York I'd miss. It's not the warm pretzels or the scenic walk to work.

It's Bennett.

If I leave now, it will be like I've pulled the shutters down on our... what did we have? A relationship? A love affair? I will have walked away from our time together. Even though I'm frustrated that he blames me for the attacks on Fort—even though if I saw him again, I'd want to shout at him for not trusting me when I've only ever given him reasons to believe in me—there's something about being in the same city, breathing the same air, that's comforting. For now. There's a pull to this city that I can't ignore.

Maybe when my heart hurts a little less, it will be easier to leave.

"I can't come back," I say. "I'll be back in a few weeks. I don't want to let Gretal down."

There's a couple of beats of silence before she says, "Your hair has grown, and it seems lighter."

"Maybe it happened in the Catskills?"

"How's Bennett?" she asks.

I haven't told her about our fight. It's unusual for me to keep information like that from my sister, but there's been so much secrecy involved in being with Bennett. Maybe that's part of the reason I'm so tired. I've been on constant guard, ensuring I don't say the wrong thing to anyone. I can't just be myself.

"Good," I say.

She must tell by my tone that something's off because her eyebrows shoot up. It's the expression she uses for the children in her care that are up to no good. "Is he the reason you're sad?" she asks.

Nothing gets past Eira. I don't know if it's the nanny in her, or the fact that she was more like a mother to me than an older sister. She knows me inside out.

"Maybe a little."

"Do I need to fly over and give him a stern talking-to?"

I laugh. I'd pay money to see how that conversation went. Bennett wouldn't stand a chance.

"No, but thanks. I'll survive. It's not like—" I can't find the words. To people looking from the outside in, it would be difficult to see how I could be cut up about what's happened to Bennett and me. Someone who didn't understand the connection I felt would tell me to move on, shake it off, get under the next guy.

I get it.

But it didn't take long for me to feel more for Bennett than I've ever felt for any man. Whatever those feelings were, they're going to take some getting over. It's not a case of slipping on some heels and a short skirt and having a night out. That's not going to cure my twisted-up insides.

Only time will do that.

I hope.

"It's not like what?" Eira asks.

"I'm twenty-two. And I'm in New York. It's not like—"

"Where did you meet him?"

This isn't a conversation I want to have. What am I going to say? *Oh, I picked him up in a bar and he shagged my brains out and I cleaned his room and he bent me over his desk.*

And then, all of a sudden, it wasn't just about sex. If it ever was.

"Work. Kinda."

"Oh, he works at the hotel?"

I need to close this conversation down. The more questions she asks, the more I reveal, the less Bennett would like it. Not that my sister knows much about Fort Inc. or American business moguls who don't want their identities revealed. Not that I couldn't trust my sister with my life. But Bennett wouldn't want to be discussed, and talking about him won't change anything.

"Sort of," I say. He does own the place. "I'm going to have a shower. And then I'm going to head to the park." It hurts, but knowing I can't have a sister-to-sister conversation about the boy who broke my heart helps a little. It makes me realize that Bennett and I were going to have to go our separate ways at some point. I can't be with someone I can't reveal to Eira. I need to start trying to move forward.

"Some sunshine and fresh air will be good for you."

"It's August in New York. Nothing about being outside is good for anyone. But I appreciate the platitude."

She laughs. "Come back home. We're due a full week of rain after today."

That's what life would be back in London. Predictably drizzly.

And Bennett-free.

Not so different to life in New York.

THIRTY-THREE

Bennett

I'm rarely nervous. I've never struggled with delivering bad news. I can't remember the last time I avoided a conversation with someone.

Today is different. This is going to be Monday night with a twist.

And the twist is, Leo's girlfriend "Nadia" is a lying, cheating thief.

Aarvi and Chul have checked and double-checked everything three times. There's no doubt about any of the information I have. I just haven't shared it with anyone yet.

All Worth, Fisher, Jack, and Byron know is that I have to deliver bad news to Leo about Nadia. I want us all to be together, although Byron can't make it as he's traveling.

Leo will need the support. And I want them all to hear what I've got to say so there's no chance of a divide in the group. Nadia lives with Leo now and there's no telling the lengths she'll go to in an effort to explain herself. I just hope Leo hears me out. I know I'm running a risk. Leo might not choose to believe me; instead, he might think I'm trying to destroy his relationship.

Worth offered his place up as neutral territory. I press the bell on the brownstone, part of me wondering whether I should have brought security.

I'm six minutes late. Enough time for everyone to have arrived before me. I'm a horrible actor, and I don't want to have to small talk with these five people who've become my family over the years. As soon as I see Leo, I want to rip off the Band-Aid.

Worth opens the door, his expression grim. He knows I wouldn't have asked for his and the others' help if this wasn't serious. At the same time, I don't want Leo thinking this is some kind of intervention or that we've all been scheming behind his back.

That's not what this is about. There should be no muddying of the waters. Everyone will find out at the same time, with me using the same words.

"Everyone's here," Worth says.

I nod. I wonder if "everyone" includes Nadia. But I don't ask. I don't want to preempt anything.

Worth and I get down to the basement and everyone turns to me in silence. They all know something's going down. They just don't know what. Thankfully, I don't see Nadia in the faces staring at me.

Worth fixes me a large whisky and Leo starts toward the sofa. I know it's time.

"Leo," I say, and he turns back to me, grinning like I'm about to tell him a joke. But this isn't going to be funny. "I need to talk to you about something."

He cocks his head and his forehead furrows slightly. The anticipation of what I'm about to say, what I'm about to do to him, is like a rusty knife in my gut.

"It's about Nadia," I say. "She's been using you to hack into my phone on Monday nights, and using my phone as a gateway into Fort Inc. We have some advanced AI capabilities that no one outside of the company knows about." I glance around. Now these five know too. "We suspect it's what she's been after."

"Fuck," Jack says over the murmurs of the other three.

"What?" Leo shakes his head. "What are you talking about?"

"You know I left my apartment because my team and I thought someone was stalking me. Apparently, it wasn't my paranoia in overdrive. Turns out it was the organization Nadia works for. They made the connection between me and Ben Fort. Found my friend group and... found a way in."

I wince as I hear how it sounds out loud. Leo was a target. A mark. A means to an end.

"I'm sorry," I say.

"Your paranoia is out of control, Bennett," Leo says. "Nadia's a model, not a fucking spy or hacker or whatever the hell you're accusing her of being."

"I get it," I reply, keeping my tone even. I don't need to add fuel to the fire I've ignited. There will be enough damage tonight, whatever happens. "It's hard to hear. And I didn't believe it at first. Partly because the way she set things up, she made it look like it was *you* trying to get through the Fort security systems."

"So you suspected me too?" he asks, his tone almost goading.

I shake my head. "Not for a second."

My phone beeps. I know it's Chul giving me an update on what's happening at Leo's apartment. He had a team go over there to keep an eye on things in case Nadia was there, and to be there when Leo found out. Just in case.

"Bennett, seriously. Have you heard yourself?" Leo asks. "This isn't a Jason Bourne movie. Nadia's not a villain."

Worth slaps Leo on the back. "Dude, Bennett's not lying to you."

His support feels like a hand on *my* back. He knows I'm not lying.

Leo turns to Worth. "You knew about this?"

Worth holds up his hands. "Absolutely not. We're all finding out at the same time. But Bennett doesn't lie. You know this. I know this. We *all* know that about Bennett. We don't lie to each other."

"But it's impossible," Leo says. "She's—I've seen her on the covers of magazines."

I shrug. That's not difficult to fake. No images are difficult to fake anymore.

He shakes his head. "There's no way. I—I—I—"

We all stand in silence, processing, allowing Leo to process.

"If it makes you feel any better, this isn't a girl and her laptop," I say. "My people think this is likely the hand of a government."

"You think it's the CIA?" Fisher asks.

I shake my head. "Not the American government or any of our allies."

"Holy fuck, Bennett. How do you get yourself into this shit?" Leo asks. My jaw slackens slightly. Does his reaction mean he's accepted what I'm saying is true?

"I'm sorry, Leo," I say.

"Fuck that. I'm sorry I let her... near you."

"This wasn't you," I reassure him. "She's... clever. I

almost didn't catch her." If it hadn't been for Efa, who knows how long it would have taken for Aarvi to tell me what she knew?

How ironic that Efa has earned a place at Fort Inc., and now that we're not together, she can take it up.

"So the entire time we were... Jeez, she's in my apartment. She's alone there now. What's she doing?" Leo asks, panic rising in his voice.

"I have a team watching your place, ready to encourage her to leave, if that's what you want," I explain.

"And when you say 'encourage her to leave,' do you mean hurl her out into the gutter?" Leo asks.

"If that's your wish," I say.

"It's not just my wish. I insist on that happening. Because if I get there and she's still there, I don't trust myself."

Which is exactly one of the reasons why I have a team there. Nadia's caused enough trouble. Leo doesn't need a criminal record as a parting gift.

"I'd like to be able to go through her things before she takes them if you don't mind?"

"Do what you like with her." He shudders. "I need a fucking shower."

"You can sleep here tonight, if you want," Worth says.

"You know I have a hotel I can stay at," Leo says, not missing an opportunity to talk about his hotel. He's definitely got something brewing there, but now's not the time to press him on it.

"I know," Worth replies. "But you might not want to stay in a hotel."

"Thank fuck I never told her about that," he says.

"I'm sorry, man," Fisher says. "I know you liked her."

Leo shakes his head, making it clear he doesn't want to

talk about it. And that's it with Leo. He comes across as this open, affable guy who's everyone's friend, but he keeps his most important cards close to his chest. Sometimes I worry about him.

"I'm fine," he says, then turns to me. "Did she get anything? Anything valuable?"

"Aarvi's pretty sure she didn't. In the end, Aarvi let her through a section of the firewall into a dummy system to try and collect some more data from her. It spooked her and... the attacks stopped."

Leo shakes his head. "I've got to stop thinking with my dick. Honestly, the sex was pretty mind-blowing." He shudders again. "I *really* gotta take a shower. Worth, man, do you mind?" He heads to the stairs, but pauses and turns back. "I'm sorry," Leo says to me, and I just shake my head.

"Don't," I say. "I brought this to your door. I'm the one who's sorry."

He takes a step toward me and we hug, silently reaffirming the bond we share. It's energy. It's forgiveness. It's life force. It's friendship through every up and down.

"I love you to your bones, man," Leo says. "I'm sorry this is happening."

Worth and Leo disappear upstairs, and I feel my body sink into the floor, heavy with relief.

It's over.

It went better than I could have hoped. Leo didn't question me—not for more than a second. Neither did any of the others. Proof, not that I needed it, that these men are more than family. We might not share the same blood, but the bond of trust between us is unbreakable.

My thoughts turn to Efa. I wish I'd afforded her the same level of trust. I haven't known her as long as the men here tonight, but she was just as loyal. I threw that loyalty away far too easily. I pushed her away and pushed her away until she disappeared. I have no one to blame but myself.

Now that the truth's uncovered, now that Leo and the rest of my circle have been told what's been going on, there's a feeling of certainty about the world being back on its rightful axis again. I feel it in every atom of my body, but peace is a distant feeling nonetheless. Up close, all I can focus on is how empty I feel, how night feels like day and day feels like night, and no matter how hot it gets in New York in August, all I can feel is ice cold since losing Efa.

THIRTY-FOUR

Efa

I have forty-five minutes for lunch. I head back into the laundry room. Daylight filters down to the basement here from a lightwell and it's one of the few places in the hotel where staff can relax *and* see daylight. I also kinda like the constant rumble of the dryers and the mountains of white towels that vary in size but never completely disappear. Somehow, it's comforting that some things are certain in this world.

I grab my book from my locker and head toward the benches where we sit when the housekeeper gives her team talks. I step over the bench so I can face the lightwell. When I crack open my book, the alarm on my phone goes off.

I check it. It's the alarm I set when we went to the Catskills to make sure we didn't sleep the entire day away. I don't know why I don't turn it off. It's a jab in the chest. Like I don't think about him enough. I don't need an alarm to bring him to mind.

It's been over two weeks since I saw him, since he questioned my loyalty and accused me of countless things I'm not capable of. On the two Monday nights since I last saw him, I couldn't stop myself from wondering whether Leo's still part of the inner circle, trying to squeeze past Fort's high walls.

Or are those walls Bennett's?

Both, maybe.

It's Tuesday lunchtime now, and I can't help but be curious about what happened last night.

My head is always so full of Fort and Leo and Bennett and Bennett and Bennett.

I hate him, and I don't, but I still absolutely miss him like crazy. I'm pissed off and frustrated that a friend of his is still getting away with what he's doing. I have so many questions. About Leo. About Fort. About Bennett. How long will it be until I stop rehearsing the list over and over in my head?

How long will it be before I have peace?

Maybe Eira was right and I should have gotten on a plane back to London weeks ago.

Even if he didn't want to listen to me, I wish Bennett had listened to Tristan or Aarvi. I'm sure his team could reassure him of Tristan's credentials.

I bring up Telegram on my phone and scan through the limited texts I had with Tristan. I type out a message, asking him for one last favor. Could he check in on Bennett? I tell him I'll pay anything that's required. First, it will prove to Bennett I'm not involved, and more importantly, Bennett will get resolution on who's trying to get into Fort's systems if he hasn't already.

As I stuff my phone back in my apron pocket, it buzzes.

Tristan's replied right away.

All sorted. Spoken to all involved and everything's resolved.

As fast as I can, I type out a reply asking for clarification, but despite staring at the phone for at least ten minutes, Tristan doesn't reply.

I pull out my book and try to read, all the while listening for another buzz, telling me Tristan's replied.

As I'm reading, the lightwell goes dark, as if someone's covered it from the sky with a great big blanket. Splatters of rain create darkened circles on the concrete floor of the lightwell.

The rain reminds me urgently of home. Ironically, these darkened skies lighten my heart. I stuff my book back in my bag and race to the staff entrance to feel the water on my face. If I could transport myself back to London with a click of my fingers right now, that's exactly what I'd do.

I burst out of the fire exit doors, away from the heat of the air-conditioning units that flank the exit, and head to the street.

I stand in my uniform on the pavement and tip my face up to the sky, enjoying the way the water lands on my face. It gives short relief to the intense heat of the middle of the day. What I give up in refreshment of air-conditioning, I get back in the feeling of home.

What am I doing in New York? I'm sure if I talk to Gretal, she'll understand I can't stay any longer. I'll find her at the end of my shift and tell her I need to resign. I've worked hard this summer and now I need to be back with my family, around people who have known me forever and loved me longer than that.

"Hey," a familiar voice says.

I open my eyes and reflexively take a step back. It's like the rain sent a mirage or something.

Bennett.

He's exactly who I'm not expecting to see.

He looks good. Tired. But he's had a haircut, and despite the heat, he's still wearing a full suit.

I'm not sorry. If this is the last image of him that I have, I'm glad he's in a suit. It's Bennett at Bennett's best.

I act like I haven't just been caught collecting raindrops on my face. "Hey," I reply.

Our gazes lock, and for a second, we're transported back to the lake, skimming stones and toasting marshmallows while debating the sense of chopping wood in lingerie. And then I remember the things he accused me of, and the doubt he had about me. My gaze falls to the ground.

"I'm sorry," he says, and I look up. "I should never have doubted you." His tone sounds genuine, but it also sounds like we had an argument last night.

It's been two weeks.

What took him so long to realize he fucked up?

"No," I say simply. "You shouldn't have." I glance back to the staff gate. I should probably get back inside. I'm not meant to be wearing my uniform on the street.

"It wasn't Leo," he says.

My gaze slices to his and I just roll my eyes. Why is he here? If he still doesn't believe me, he should just keep that to himself from now on. I've heard enough.

"I'm serious," he continues. "Aarvi and her team figured it out. It was Nadia. She was making it look like Leo to cover her tracks."

"Nadia?" I ask. And things start to slot into place. It makes much more sense for it to be an outsider than one of Bennett's closest friends. He's so careful and cautious about the people he surrounds himself with. They are more like brothers than friends. It was as if they had surrounded themselves with an invisible ring of steel that nothing could permeate. It makes much more sense that Bennett got that right.

I sigh, breathing out some of the frustration that's been building over the last two weeks. "That's good." I pause. "For you. I mean, it's good that Leo is who you thought he was."

Bennett nods and pushes his hands into his pockets. "I should have trusted you."

"Yeah, well, I was wrong about Leo."

"But you had my best interests at heart."

I let out a sour laugh. "Yeah, I did."

"I'm not good at trusting people."

"Really?" I ask, tone mocking. "I hadn't noticed."

"Can I make it up to you?"

"How?" I ask.

"Maybe I can come over tonight? Or we can have dinner. We could go to my club?"

A wave of fatigue washes over me. "And we can hide out from the world?"

He narrows his eyes in confusion.

"Bennett, I'm happy you've discovered that I wasn't your hacker and that Leo wasn't either. I'm glad you've found who's done it. And I'm pleased to see you. I've missed you..." I look away because it's too intense. "I've missed you too much. But this is done."

"Done?" he asks. "So you don't forgive me?" He sighs. "I understand. But I'll make it up to you. I'm too used to people with nefarious intentions. I'm sorry you got caught up in my issues with that."

"I do forgive you," I reply. "I forgive you, but it doesn't mean we get to restart what we had."

I'm not sure what I'm saying. I thought it was my anger

at him distrusting me that would keep us apart if he ever came back. But I truly forgive him. I'm not angry anymore. I'm glad he doesn't think badly of me. I can walk away in peace.

He searches my face like he's looking for clues.

I get it. It's not fair. I've not just changed the goalposts on him. I've changed the game.

I'm in love with the man in front of me. And that means I have to walk away. Because if he comes any closer, I don't know if I'll have the strength to leave. And I know I should.

I can't have a life where I'm hiding out, not going to dinner, not enjoying our life together out in the open. I want to be able to complain to my sister and whoever's around me about my man. I want to be able to tell people where my boyfriend works and what he does for a living.

I don't want to be treading on lies everywhere I stand.

"I care about you," I continue. "But maybe it was for the best that things ended when they did."

"So you don't forgive me, then?" He sounds confused and frustrated.

"You called me a liar once already. How did that work out for you?" I ask him. The rain has stopped now, and I can almost see the steam come up from the streets as the sun sucks up the rain, storing it, waiting for the next storm. The water cycle up close and personal. I don't want to be caught in a cycle of wanting something different from what Bennett's offering and getting frustrated when he can't give me more.

"I don't get it," he says. "If you forgive me, then..."

"Then what? That's exactly where my mind went too. Then what? So you come over tonight, so we slip back into the easiness between us. And then what?"

I search his face. If he has answers, I'll take them. If

there's a way of clearing the path in front of us, I want to hear it.

"Then I go back to London—that's a huge elephant in the room. But let's jump over that one. Say I don't go back. Say I stay. And I'm in New York, then what? Who do I tell my sister I'm staying in New York for? Are you Bennett Fordham or Ben Fort or another alias? And where do you work and who was your mother?"

His eyes are filled with confusion.

"I won't live with lies and half-truths. I don't want to conceal and hide. Life is complicated enough. I'm only twenty-one, and my life has been filled with bumps and bends and... I like simple. I like the truth. And as much as I like you... as much as I care, I don't want to get into this any deeper when I know there will be a time when I have to say goodbye. The last two weeks have been difficult enough."

It's almost impossible to be so close to him, yet not be able to touch him. For me not to feel his hand in my hair and his lips on my forehead. I want to drink in the scent that permeates every jacket he wears.

But I have to be strong.

I can't live the life with Bennett that he requires. I can't live a life of lies.

"So the problem isn't Leo, and me not trusting you—"

Our gazes lock. I will him to understand what I'm about to tell him. "I told you I forgive you and I mean it. You made a mistake. We haven't known each other long. I know who you are." I place my palm over his chest and I'm seconds away from melting into his heat. His hardness. "You're a good man. I know it's difficult for you to trust people. I'm telling you I understand, and I forgive you. I'm not making you pay a penance. I'm trying to save both of us... save myself from more pain down the road."

There's a huge non-negotiable boulder in the middle of our road together. Better that we know now than continue to speed along and crash headfirst later on.

"So that's it?" he says. "Your mind is made up?"

"It's not about me making up my mind. The evidence is all laid out—we've collected all the data. You have non-negotiables in your world. I have them in mine. And they don't mesh."

Sadness cloaks his face, and I wish I had the power to wash it away. I hate to see him hurting, but I can't live by his rules. I wish I could.

"What can I do?" he asks.

I give a small shake of my head. "There's nothing to be done."

He closes his eyes as if he's trying to shut out the pain. Even though it hurts that he hurts, there's comfort in knowing he cares. That whatever we had between us was mutual.

"I'm going to miss you," I say.

He opens his eyes and his expression is pleading. But I know I can't soothe him. Not without losing everything that's important to me.

The alarm on my phone sounds. Lunchtime is over.

"I have to go," I say, and my voice breaks.

I take him in, one last vision I'll always treasure—my first love. And I turn and leave.

THIRTY-FIVE

Bennett

I take a seat on the low rust-colored couches at Leo's private members club. He's sitting opposite me. Neither of us is talking.

I don't have the energy to speak. Just existing takes everything I have at the moment.

The last three weeks without Efa have been some of the hardest of my life. Logically, it makes no sense. I'd never met the woman before the start of this summer. It's been just weeks but I'm beginning to realize I've been forever altered by her. I wonder if I'll ever actually get over not having her in my life.

All I see when I close my eyes is her standing in front of me outside the hotel, telling me she doesn't want to be with me.

I take a sip of my drink and squeeze my eyes shut, not because I'm trying to stop thinking about her, but because I know it will be her that I see when I do.

"Hey," Worth's voice says from behind me.

I lift up my drink and nod. I don't know why I came tonight. I'm not much company at the moment. But maybe that's why I'm here.

"Oh god," he says. "You two look pathetic." He takes a seat next to me and gives his drink order to the waiter.

"Noted," I say.

"Uncle Fisher's here!" I turn to see Fisher heading over to us.

The club is quiet, probably because Leo insisted we have the entire floor to ourselves. Although ESPN is on, it's muted. On our group chat, he said he never wants to see another woman again. I have to admit, it was the first time I've smiled for weeks. I'm not happy Leo's miserable, but he's had enough women to last him a lifetime. I doubt his abstinence will last long.

"It's all going to be okay," Fisher says. "Oh, and Byron's not coming again. Something came up apparently."

Hardly a surprise. I'm not sure what's going on with Byron at the moment. I probably should have checked in with him, but there's been so much going on this summer.

Jack appears from out of nowhere and it's the five of us. "So what's on the agenda tonight?" Jack asks.

Booze. Sleep. Misery.

I tip back my head, empty my glass, and slide it onto the table.

"Okay," Worth says. "I'll be in charge of the agenda. First, no driving home."

I nod. That I can agree to. I can take a taxi back to the Mandarin Oriental, where I've been staying since I left The Avenue.

"Second, we'll deal with Leo. Third, Bennett."

"No," I snap. "There's nothing wrong with me."

Worth doesn't respond, just turns to Leo. "Okay, so how are things with you?"

"Great," Leo deadpans. "The only woman I've let in and it hasn't been all about sex uses me to get to my best friend. Life is peachy."

I catch Jack's wince. Worth pulls in a breath.

"That's bullshit," I say.

"What's bullshit?" Leo asks.

"The part where you say you let the woman in."

"She moved in, Bennett. She cooked me dinner and we —" He sighs. "Never mind."

"That doesn't mean you let her in." I know because I let Efa in. More than anyone.

"Bennett's right," Worth says. "Just because she had her panties in the drawer next to yours doesn't mean you were emotionally invested."

"I don't wear panties," Leo snaps, and I can't help but let out a laugh. A small smile curls around Leo's mouth.

Worth rolls his eyes. "You know what I mean."

"Look," Leo says. "I like women—I've never tried to deny it. But I did think that Nadia might be... different."

You'd know, you wouldn't think. I don't say it, because he doesn't want to hear it from me. But he would have known if Nadia was special. It wouldn't be in doubt.

"Maybe you were hoping she would be," Worth says. "Maybe different is what you're looking for?"

Leo shakes his head. "Absolutely not. I'll be okay," he says. "I'll spend a couple of days licking my wounds. I'll move and I'll be right back to business as usual."

"You'll move?" Jack asks. "What do you mean?"

"There's no fucking way I'm staying in that apartment. Jesus Christ, I've had to have twenty showers a day for the last week. My fucking skin is falling off. I'm not putting myself through staying there, where she was spying on me and my friends. No way. I've been staying at the hotel since last Monday." He lifts his chin toward me. "Bennett had the right idea moving into his hotel. I've already come up with some revenue-generating projects for the place."

Leo will be okay. I have no doubt about it. He's one of the strongest men I know.

"You're going to find a new apartment?" I ask.

"I have a meeting with a realtor tomorrow. We'll see what's out there."

"That sounds positive," Worth says. "Maybe you could think about whether part of the reason you had Nadia move in was because you wanted something more than..."

"The field of gorgeous women that is New York City?" Leo rolls his eyes. "Nah. I just need to bench myself for a minute. I'll be back in the game in no time."

Worth might be onto something with Leo, but now's not the time and Worth gets it. He doesn't push.

"Anyone got anything pressing they want to raise?" Worth asks

"Are we at Monday night sports or a board meeting?" Leo asks.

"I apologized to Efa for not believing her and for not trusting her," I confess.

"Great," Worth says. "Are things back on track for you two now?"

I groan. "Nope."

"Don't worry about it," Fisher says. "She'll come around." Most things work out for Fisher, so he can't possibly comprehend the idea of life not going his way. I envy him.

"Will she come around?" Worth asks.

I shake my head and beckon over the waiter. There isn't enough whisky in the world.

"Have you thought about buying her a really expensive gift? Like a necklace or a watch or something?" Fisher asks. "In my experience, a nice gift can get you out of most situations with women."

It takes effort not to roll my eyes. Fisher is being ridiculous. If he's spending time with women who are won over by expensive gifts, he's spending time with the wrong women.

"This isn't a situation that can be fixed with a new watch," I say.

"What about a car?" he suggests.

Worth glares at him. "She won't forgive you?"

I let out a resigned laugh. "If only it were that simple. She forgave me. Quickly. Graciously. And without any expensive gifts. It was more than I deserved."

"So what's the problem?" Fisher asks.

"I'm the problem," I reply. "The way I like things so private. Discreet."

"Right," they all chorus in unison, like they all completely understand where she's coming from.

"So we're done," I explain.

"Just like that?" Worth asks. I shrug. "And I'm guessing from... your mood, that you'd prefer not to be done."

"Of course." I want to go home every night and slide into bed next to her. I want to pull her against me and smell her scent that's peaches and earth at the same time. I want to feel what it's like to have her belly laugh when I say something, even though it was just a little bit funny. I want to hold her when she's sad and I want to hear every thought inside her head.

"But it's impossible. I understand she doesn't want to...

hide, or hide me, or have to lie—I get it. She was surrounded by lies for a long time."

"Are you technically lying?" Fisher says. "I mean, your name is Bennett Fordham."

"Right. But I'm not open about being at the helm of Fort Inc. I'm not open about being the son of Kathleen Fordham. You five know those things about me. She knows those things about me."

"You told her who your mom was?" Worth asks.

"I did."

"Wow," Fisher says.

"Precisely," Jack says. "Wow. How did you feel?"

"Fine. Good, even. Telling her was like a weight lifted."

"Did she know who she was? Efa's young."

"She knew. Reeled off her favorite movies and—"

"You were okay with that?" Worth asks.

I huff out a laugh. "Yeah. I liked the fact she knew of Kathleen Fordham. It was... more of a connection or something."

"That's big, Bennett," Leo says. "I didn't realize that she... you two were so close."

I nod, unable to speak, because I have a lump of rock biting into the flesh of my throat.

We *were* close.

"And so she just walked away?" Fisher says.

"It's easier this way," I say. "There's no point in spending more time together if things are going to end at some point." Except I would have liked more time.

Even if it meant more pain in the long run.

"It's her decision."

"You sound broken," Fisher says.

"It's rough. But I'll bounce back, just like Leo." Except it's different. Efa wasn't Nadia. She didn't betray me. Quite the opposite. And I understand that she doesn't want to betray herself and her own needs and boundaries. I respect that about her. I love that about her.

I love *her*.

I'm not sure I'll ever bounce back from loving her.

"You don't think she's worth fighting for?" Fisher asks.

"I don't have anything left to fight with," I say. "I can't give her what she needs."

"But can't you?" Worth asks. "It sounds like you have a choice: Efa or your anonymity."

"It's not like she's asking you to announce it in *Forbes*," Fisher says. "Is she?"

"She hasn't asked me for anything," I reply. "She knows there's no point."

"Changing your name after your mom died. I get it," Worth says. "You wanted to get out from under her shadow and become a person in your own right. You didn't trust people who knew you as her son, because she was surrounded by people who were there because of her fame and fortune. But, now?" He frowns, but I'm not sure why. "Now? You've carved out a piece of this world for yourself. No one is just going to see you as her son. And it doesn't matter if you're Ben Fort or Bennett Fordham, people are going to fawn. They're going to want to be close to you because you have money and success. It's the same for all of us. It's our job to spot those people and only trust those we know are genuine."

Leo raises his hand. "Don't come to me for lessons."

I smirk. Leo's down, but he's not out. Never in this lifetime.

"So what, you think I should just rip open my shirt and announce I'm Batman?"

I'm met with a round of jeers. "That's just weird,"

Fisher says. "You're not Batman. You're just an uptight businessman who's overly paranoid."

I actually manage to smile at that one. "You make it sound so simple. But it's not. I've spent a long time building walls around me, and I come back and strengthen them all the time. I am surrounded by people who respect me—not my fame or my reputation, but my work. My character. Who I am."

"Exactly," Worth says. "You've done the hard work. Now's the time to reap what you've sown."

I pull in a breath at the idea that I could let go of these reins that I've been holding on to so tightly for so long.

"I'm not sure where I'd start, or even if I want to," I confess.

"You have to decide whether Efa's worth it," Leo says.

Leo's statement is all it takes for the fog to lift and everything to become clear. Because I know that Efa's worth everything I can give her.

THIRTY-SIX

Efa

I press the button on the lift to take me to the Park Suite for the very last time. It's fitting that this room will be the last one I service. It's Marcella's day off and I'm filling in. I'm no longer the newbie who needs to be shown how to fold the loo paper. I stack my trolley in record time, I have a shortcut for fitting the maximum amount of shortbread biscuits to the assigned container, and I manage to hook my vacuum cleaner to the trolley like it's a trailer. I'm a pro. Trained by the best.

Gretal's agreed for me to leave early. Next weekend will be Labor Day and apparently the hotel's always quiet. I can slip off back to London like I was never here. Only two things have changed. I've accepted I'm never going to be an employee of Fort Inc., and actually, I quite like tech security. It's a growth industry, and I like the idea of protecting people and assets. This summer, I've tried it on like brand-new shoes, and now, as the season end approaches, they're so soft and comfortable, I don't want to give them up.

Tristan works alone, but I'm not like that. I want to work with people, and so I've sent off applications to three companies in the UK. I'm waiting to hear back. I might not have any certainty, but it feels like there's a path forward. I just need to follow it.

The light to make up the Park Suite is on and I pull out the master key from my pocket and knock on the door. When there's no answer, I click open the lock. "Housekeeping," I call. It's dark. The curtains are still pulled, and I flick on the lights before heading into the bathroom.

It doesn't look like it's been touched. I'm used to people not using the shower or the bath. I'm still not over it, because why in the hell aren't people washing regularly, but I'm not used to the towels still being in place and the soaps and mirrors all being as good as new. I pull out my tablet. Maybe I've made a mistake and this room isn't on the list for servicing.

I scroll up and find it last on my list. Room is listed as checked out. Maybe they had other plans? I head into the sitting area to see if anything else has been touched, but it looks good as new. The bedroom too. The bed hasn't been slept in.

It's like my own personal leaving present—my last room, the most important room, doesn't need to be serviced. I just saved myself ninety minutes. Somebody must have failed to check in last night.

And then my gaze catches on the curtains. The turn-down team must have been in last night, so I need to reset for a daytime check-in. I set to work, undoing the turndown by changing where the water is kept and moving the remote control, opening the curtains and returning the slippers to the dressing room. I double back into the bathroom and see that the bathmat has been set out, as is always the case in a turndown, and I hang it back up.

I turn three hundred and sixty degrees, sweeping my gaze up to the ceiling and down to the floor so I make sure everything's in place.

Bathroom done. Then I head to the bedroom for a final check.

Bedroom done.

As I'm heading through the bedroom area, my gaze snags on the desk. My stomach flips at the memory of Bennett behind me, my uniform pushed up to my waist.

That's when I see it.

A magazine.

Most of the magazines are set out on the coffee table as per hotel protocol. One of the turndown team must have missed it and I need to put it back. I reach for the magazine and it takes me a second, maybe two or three, to understand what I'm seeing.

It's *Forbes*, but it's marked as a special edition.

The headline reads, "The Most Powerful Man in Tech: Unmasked."

There's no doubt who's staring back at me from the cover.

Bennett.

My eye goes to the top of the cover, to the bottom, looking for a date, but there isn't one. What's happening? Is this a mock-up? Something he's had created just for me? There's a newsstand just along from the hotel and I step toward the window, seeing if I can make it out. I'm not sure what I'm expecting to see from up here. Even if this was an actual copy of *Forbes*, it's not like the newsstand is going to have it stapled to the roof.

I run my fingers over the picture of Bennett's face, then

flick open the front page. I'm not an avid reader of *Forbes*, but it looks legit. All over, it's stamped special edition and it's not as thick as the copies I've picked up from time to time, but other than that, it looks the same.

I skip the contents page and land on another image of Bennett. This one's a picture of him behind a desk, dressed in his suit, looking serious and seriously sexy.

It has been so hard to stay away from him these last days. On most evenings, I've been so close to calling him, going to him, desperate to feel his fingers hooked over my hips, his lips on my neck, his laugh in my chest.

I've been willing all thoughts of him away, but he seems to follow me. Even into empty hotel rooms.

The article is an interview with Bennett. I collapse back into the office chair and start reading. He talks about the reasons he's been so secretive. He speaks openly about all the things he clearly found it so difficult to tell me. The price his mom paid for fame. His concerns for her. Kathleen's death, and how that led to a rebirth. How he didn't want to have the life she did, wanted to build something from the ground up.

I'm confused. I don't understand whether this is a public interview or whether he's created this magazine just for me. I'm not quite sure what he's trying to say.

I keep reading, and it's so nice to hear his voice in the answers to the questions. The intelligence, the wit. The unrelenting charm.

And then he's asked a final question: Why is he coming forward now, after all these years protecting his identity so fiercely?

"I realize I can't have the personal life I want without being more open."

"That's cryptic," the interviewer says. "Tell us more

about your personal life. Are you an eligible bachelor or a happily married man?"

"I've met the woman I want to spend the rest of my life with," he answers.

My heart disintegrates in my chest.

He's done this for me. I know for certain that this isn't some weird mock-up. He's given this interview to *Forbes*.

My phone buzzes, and I already know before I have it in my hand that it's Bennett.

It's an email with just a link attached.

It's the interview online. He knew I'd doubt whether it was public.

I stand and glance around. I'm not sure what I'm supposed to do now. I clutch the magazine to my chest and head out.

The Park Suite is ready for its next guest, and I'm no longer a member of staff at The Avenue. This chapter is over, and I'm ready to move on to the next.

THIRTY-SEVEN

Bennett

It's five after five and I've been sitting at this bar for two hours. All I can do is wait. After two virgin mojitos, I'm pretty sure the bartender thinks I'm an alcoholic trying to resist the urge to drink. I need a clear head for what happens next.

I glance up and Gretal comes toward me. "Bennett, I didn't know you were in the hotel."

Just after I sat down with *Forbes*, I stopped by the hotel and introduced myself to Gretal. No more hiding. No more lies. That's what Efa needs, and I need her. So here we are.

"It's not an official visit. As I said, things won't change for you."

She laughs. "Maybe in your eyes, but when the owner of the hotel is on the premises, I like to know."

Which is why I never wanted her to. But it's a price I'm willing to pay.

"How's the season been?" I ask her.

"Wild," she replies. "Lots of ups and downs. The

vomiting bug was a low point. But we made it. Bookings are up compared to this time last year."

"Good. At some point, I'd like to sit down with you and go through what I learned as a guest."

Gretal's wide smile doesn't falter. I don't get the impression she's the kind of person who is easily ruffled. She's good at her job and she knows it, which is exactly how it should be. "I'd welcome that. Having a secret shopper is always helpful."

"Am I right in thinking you're relatively new to hotels?"

"Yeah, I was in PR before. Reputation management mainly."

"You didn't like it?"

She laughs. "It had its moments. I had the strange idea that I'd come to New England and open a bed-and-breakfast. I worked on a concept for a new resort for... well, I'll save that for another time. Point is, I'm here now, running a hotel. It's not quite what I planned, but that's okay."

"I think you're a great leader. If the time comes when you're looking for new opportunities, I want to be the first person you tell."

She pauses, her brows pinching a little. "Thanks. I appreciate that." She silences the buzz of the radio attached to her waist.

"You have my number," I say, "if you need anything."

She lifts her chin slightly. "And vice versa. Enjoy your cocktail."

I check the time on my phone. I know Efa's shift finished at five and I can't help but wonder if she'll call.

Was it too little, too late?

I can only hope I've done enough.

"Can I get another mocktail?" I say to the bartender. "I don't care which one. I can't read the menu anyway." It may be light outside, but in this bar, it's always a step away from pitch black. I can't wait to get Gretal to change that.

"A virgin Vagabond Shoes, coming right up," he says, just as I get a tap on my shoulder.

I don't need to turn around to see who it is.

I know.

Relief anchors my body to my chair, and I turn.

"I'm looking for a guy who just blew up his life for me." Her eyes are sparking like tiny fireworks.

"You read it?" I ask, sliding off my stool.

"Of course I read it."

"And you got my email."

"Of course I got your email. And I overhead Gretal telling someone how you blindsided her by announcing you owned the hotel and have been staying in the Park Suite for weeks."

"No more pretending to be anyone other than who I am. And who I am is a man in love with you."

She reaches up and cups my face. Relief and hope and joy bloom deep in my gut. "I love you too." She glances to the floor. "I never expected this from you. I didn't ask you—"

"I know you didn't ask. I want you. I want you more than my anonymity. I want you more than anything else in the world. So I did what it took. Was it enough?"

She nods, and I wrap my arms around her, reveling in her softness. It feels so right, so exactly where I'm supposed to be.

Now. Tomorrow. Forever.

"Looks like New York has me a little longer than a summer," she says.

"You're going to stay?" I ask, my heart lifting in my

chest. I thought we were just over the first hurdle. Her living on a different continent was our next test.

"I'm wherever you are," she responds, and I pull her closer. "If you're in New York, I'm in New York. These last few weeks without you..." She shakes her head a little like she's trying to shake off a memory. "I don't want to do that again. I don't want to be anywhere you're not. And these feelings are new to me. I know I haven't had a lot of experience in relationships, but it feels too important to walk away from."

I press a kiss to her forehead. "For what it's worth, I don't have too much more experience in relationships, either. But I know you're too important to walk away from. And I won't. Not ever. Not as long as you want me to stay."

Her eyes go wide. "Forever?"

I nod. "That's what I'm saying."

She slides her hands up my chest and lifts up on her tiptoes. "Forever."

I slide my hands up her back and sweep my lips over hers, savoring the moment. This is the last woman I'll ever kiss, and I can't wait to begin forever with her.

Efa's mine now. She's the woman I gave up my anonymity for. And I'll happily keep giving up whatever she needs me to, now and until the end of time.

THIRTY-EIGHT

Efa

We walk into Ben's suite at the Mandarin Oriental, and my gaze is immediately drawn to the gold-leaf ceiling. "You know you're cheating on your own hotel by staying here."

"Market research," Bennett says. "I just couldn't go back to my apartment."

"But Nadia's been caught. And anyway, you're on the cover of *Forbes*. I hate to tell you but your cover is officially blown." I grin at him, and then can't *stop* grinning, because being with him, knowing we have a future together, feels almost too good to be true.

"I know. It's not that. I just don't want to go backward, you know?"

I narrow my eyes at him. "Do I?"

"I chose my old apartment because I was hiding. It was an out-of-the-way building with a private entrance. The security is unrivaled. It doesn't seem like a place I belong anymore. A place *we* belong."

How did this guy go from dickwad to mushball?

How did I turn into this heart-eyed gal who's prepared to emigrate for a guy?

"A place we belong?" I exhale and try to imagine what it will be like living in New York. "My sister isn't going to be happy that where I belong isn't next door to her in London. You know my brother-in-law lives opposite his brother."

"I can't wait to meet all these brothers-in-law. If they even exist."

I laugh. "You'll meet them. We'll have to go over at some point. I actually need to call my sister and fill her in on all the bits I've not told her."

"All the bits?"

"Like how I'm in love with this reclusive tech billionaire and he's making me stay stateside."

He flops down next to me on the sofa and reaches for my waist. "Get your cell. Let's call her now. No time like the present."

"It's eleven. I'm not sure she'll even be up."

"Then we'll leave a message."

A flutter of excitement skates over my skin. I love that he's so willing to meet my sister. "Okay." I bring up my phone and start a video call to Eira.

She answers on the first ring. "Hey! How was your last day?"

I wince. She's so looking forward to me coming home. "Well, I have a funny story to tell you."

I glance over at Bennett, who's grinning at me. I reach up and cup his jaw, swiping his chin with my thumb. "I might not be coming back tomorrow as planned."

"What? But I miss you! Did you get a job at Fort?"

Bennett and I lock eyes. "Better than that." I press my lips together, scared about what I'm about to admit. "I'm in love with the CEO, and I'm really hoping that he's going to marry me."

"What?" she screams.

Dax shushes her in the background. Poor Guinevere. I hope she didn't get woken up.

"Are you kidding?" she asks.

Bennett shifts so he's in frame. "Hi, Eira. Nice to meet you."

"Oh wow, you're not kidding," Eira says. "But you were joking about the marriage thing, right? You're twenty-one."

"If she wants to wait, we can wait," Bennett says. "But married or not, we're together now. I want to be with her for the rest of my life." I lean into Bennett, trying to get closer. Will I ever not want to be as close to him as possible?

Eira turns, and I can tell she's looking at Dax. Knowing him, he's not following what's going on. He's probably focused on a medical journal or something.

"It's still you and me and Dylan," I say, my voice breaking. Bennett takes the phone from me, keeping the screen on me but freeing up my hands. "Just like when you found Dax and Guinevere. Being with Bennett doesn't change that."

"Except you're so far away." This time it's Eira's voice that cracks.

"If you think about it, it's just like living in Scotland and coming up and down on the train. It's only a six- or seven-hour flight." Before I can tell her how I can come back to London periodically, Dax comes into the shot.

"What are you doing tomorrow?" he asks. He probably wants to get to bed and have this conversation another time. Except I don't want to leave my sister upset.

I look at Bennett and then back to the screen. "I'm not doing anything. I've finished at work, so I'm not making beds. Bennett and I have only just... you know, we haven't planned anything."

"Okay, so we'll see you tomorrow around lunchtime your time," Dax says bluntly, like I live in Notting Hill and we're meeting at a local café. "I've just texted Vincent and we can borrow the jet—not the first time I've asked him for that particular favor, and it won't be the last if I have a sister-in-law in New York."

"What?" Eira says.

I half squeal, half yelp. "Did I tell you, you're my favorite brother-in-law?"

"You don't need to tell me. Of course I am."

"We'll get to meet you in person, Bennett," Eira says.

"Saw the *Forbes* thing," Dax says, as if he's just mentioned it's raining. "Eddie's the one you mention, right?"

"Yup," Bennett says.

"You went public for her?" Dax asks.

"Yup," Bennett asks.

"Yeah, Eira, he'll do for Eddie." He presses a kiss to the side of her head. "Eddie, I'll talk to Eira. And we'll see you tomorrow. Everything's going to be fine."

And that's why I love Dax for my sister.

"Thanks, Dax. Love you, Eira."

Eira blows me a kiss and we hang up.

"I don't have a jet," Bennett says as I toss my phone on the table in front of us.

"Your takeaway from that conversation is that you don't have a jet?" I link my fingers through his and press a kiss to the back of his hand.

"It just got me thinking, that's all. It might be a good idea to get one."

I groan. "No. Think of the environmental cost. We can fly like normal people."

"You mean charter something?" he asks.

I shake my head. "You're ridiculous. We can go online, book a seat, and turn up to the airport like everyone else."

"I'm not sure about that." He bends and presses a kiss on the corner of my mouth. "How am I going to fuck you on a commercial flight?"

"Maybe you're not going to fuck me on a commercial flight. Ever thought about that?"

He leans over me, and my entire body flushes with heat. "You're mine now."

"I was always yours," I reply. I don't know what it was about Bennett that first time I met him. He wasn't the first man I'd ever slept with, but in so many ways it felt like he was. Maybe that's how everyone feels when they meet the love of their life. I felt it then, and every time he's touched me since.

He growls. "It's been too long."

"I was in physical pain being away from you," I say, lifting my arms as he peels my top off.

He strokes his knuckles down my cheek and shakes his head. "Never again. I'm serious about marrying you. I don't have a ring and I haven't gone down on one knee, but I will."

I pull at his shirt, trying to get the buttons open as quickly as I can. I don't want to wait any longer to feel his skin against mine.

"I know. And I'm going to say yes. But maybe we can just do something small, with those closest to us. My sister is going to do a big wedding next year and... I just need you."

"Whatever you want," he says, shifting so he's kneeling on the floor between my thighs. "I've got to taste you again."

There's no preamble before he sinks his tongue into me like he's been deprived for too long and now he's going to feast.

I open my legs wider, wanting to give him everything I have.

THIRTY-NINE

Bennett

I can't remember a time when I felt this content. And it's not just because I'm face-deep in Efa's pussy right now, although that's part of it.

Being with her feels like a kind of right I didn't know existed. Being close to her feels like home. Holding her hand makes me feel like I belong to some exclusive club of two that no one else can possibly imagine. Just the scent of her brings to mind playfulness, like summer peaches and water fountains. She brings levity to my life that I didn't realize I needed. Not that she's not serious. She is. She's clever and insightful and completely and utterly unafraid. I not only love her, but I respect her, I revere her. I worship this woman. She. Is. Everything.

She bucks off the sofa and shudders beneath me.

It's not just a deep sense of satisfaction I feel at making her come, it's also the utter bliss at the thought I'm going to be doing that for the rest of our lives.

I get to taste her forever.

I get to have her forever.

I get to love her forever.

I take the rest of my clothes off, lift her from the sofa and carry her into the bedroom. She should be comfortable. We have a long night ahead of us. It's the start of a long life together.

She pulls at my shoulders.

"I want you close."

I close my eyes in a long blink, savoring her words. I want her close too.

I move over her and press a kiss to her lips. Instantly she deepens it, pressing her tongue against mine, tasting and teasing. Her hand slides up my side and my skin sheets in goose bumps. How can just a simple touch from her have such a huge effect on me?

I settle over her, our hips locked together, my length against her, waiting while we touch and taste. I dip and take a nipple into my mouth, sucking and pulling and grazing my teeth against her as she moans, circling her hips, wanting more but everything just as it is as well.

I understand what she's feeling because I'm feeling it too: need.

"I don't want to get pregnant," she says, panic in her tone.

I pause and gaze at her. "Ever?" I ask. We haven't had these fundamental conversations, but it doesn't matter, because I want everything she wants. I want her to be happy.

"Yet. And for a few years."

"Okay," I say.

"But we need condoms," she says. "Lot and lots of condoms."

I smirk. "We have enough. We can get more."

"You might have to buy a condom factory."

"I'll buy a condom factory," I reassure her.

She nods, like an imminent condom shortage has been a serious concern to her.

I reach across to the nightstand and grab a condom from my wallet.

"Condom," I say, holding it up.

"Bennett," she cries out. "Please. Quickly."

I clench my jaw at her impatience. It's like she's going to boil over if I don't get inside her as quickly as possible. Sheathed, I press my crown over her folds. I'm not sure if I'm teasing her or torturing myself. She just feels so good.

"You ready?" I ask. I'm a dick for teasing her. She's so wet, her body is vibrating with yearning. She's more than ready and she knows I know.

She twists her hips, trying to get closer, but I pull back. This time it's not to tease. This time it's to steady myself. To prepare for the feeling of her around me.

But it's hopeless.

When I push into her, the delicious clench of her makes me dizzy with desire. With one simple movement, I'm so close to the edge, I need to focus on her fingernails digging into my back to keep me from falling.

Her breathy whimpers don't help.

"It's so much," she cries out, and I close my eyes, trying to wrestle some control back.

I start to move and groan. The pull, the drag, the grip she has around me. In every way, it's more than I've ever known. My pulse pounds in my ears. Heat turns to sweat across my brow and down my back but I don't stop, I can't stop.

We move together, hip to hip, mouth to tongue, fingers

to flesh. It's physical, but it's a beginning, a ceremony at the start of something.

"Fuck, Efa," I choke out.

"I'm here," she says, her fingers in my hair.

Those words are what finally tip me over the edge and I know there's no going back. My vision flashes white and I feel her orgasm shatter through her as mine races through me, pulling the air from my lungs and the strength from my hands.

"I need more," she says, still fighting for breath. "More of you." Her delicate fingers push at my shoulders, and from somewhere I find the energy to roll from where I'm lying on top of her to the side.

She arranges herself so she's astride me and pulls her hair up behind her, before letting it fall over her shoulders again. Her breasts rise and fall and I reach for them, teasing her nipples between my thumbs and forefingers, my dick already hardening at the show I'm getting.

She's like a fucking wet dream come to life.

Moving her hips, she slides her folds down my dick, bringing life to me again.

Her eyes slide to mine. "Again," she says. It might be the sexiest thing she's ever said to me.

I'm not about to start disappointing my soon-to-be wife.

"So greedy."

She lifts her chin. "Fuck me, Bennett."

She doesn't have to ask me again.

I lift her up and off me, arranging her legs over the side of the bed. I stand behind her and press her down. I slide a new condom on and push into her. Quickly this time, without waiting. If my woman wants to get fucked, then who am I to deny her.

I thrust into her and the force of my movement pushes her down onto the bed.

"Ass up," I say. She complies and moves back so I can hook my fingers under her hips and thrust again.

And again.

And again.

"You're going to be sore tomorrow," I say matter-of-factly. "I'm going to have you so many times tonight, you're not going to be able to stand."

Her hands grip the bedcovers and her breaths come heavy.

I dip under her hips and my fingers find her clit. She lets out a muffled scream.

But I don't want her stopping herself from making all the noise she wants.

I push harder and deeper and circle around and around. She reaches back for my arm, and I can't tell if she's trying to stop me or she just needs to feel me.

"Bennett," she cries out. "Bennett."

My name on her lips when she's at her most vulnerable, when she's on the edge of climax like this, has me spiraling into bliss.

I'm the luckiest man alive to have this woman under me, screaming my name. My orgasm rumbles in the distance and I can't stop. Don't want to. Efa comes apart under me, in my hands, and I shove into her one final time, my head back, her name ripped from my throat in celebration.

Like I said: I'm the luckiest man alive.

EPILOGUE

Two weeks later

Bennett

Life with Efa is so different to my life without her. For a start, she has us going to visit places with unpronounceable names.

"Nor-fuck," I say.

She pulls her mouth wide and wrinkles her nose. "No. Please don't say Nor-fuck. You sound so American."

"I *am* American."

"How did I fall in love with you?" She laughs and shakes her head like she's the most ridiculous person on the planet for loving me. It doesn't faze me at all. I know she loves me hard. So hard I can't believe how lucky I am.

"So tell me again," I say. "We have the exact same spelling for a place in the US. I don't understand why we can't all get together and agree on a pronunciation."

"Nor-ferk. It's an 'errr' sound. Not a 'u.'"

"And you don't pronounce the L? Just like our Norfolk?"

She shrugs. "Come on. No judging, please. We've been developing the English language since the fifth century. You guys have had it for a few hundred years. Get over yourself."

I chuckle "Norferk it is," I say.

Her eyes light up like I already gave her the diamond ring I have in my pocket. "Yes! Just like that."

"Well, if you say it has the best sky in the world, then it must be worth visiting... despite its weird name."

"Yeah, it really is wonderful. I only started coming because this is where Dax's parents are; I told you, the family has kind of adopted Eira, Dylan, and me." She squeals. "Speaking of—there's Carole, Dax's mum."

We pull into the driveway of what looks like a small hotel with a gravel drive and park. An older woman wearing an apron with images of a man's face on it races toward us.

"My darling Eddie," she says, cupping Efa's face as soon as she gets close enough. Her eyes go glassy. "I'm so happy for you."

I shut the car door and round the hood to meet them.

"You must be Bennett. What a pleasure it is to have you here."

"And you must be Mrs. Cove," I say.

She rolls her eyes and takes my hand in hers. She turns to Efa. "Americans. Always so formal." Then she turns back to me. "We don't stand on ceremony here. Call me Carole." She nods over to the other side of the large driveway. "That's my husband, John. John!" she calls out. "Come and say hello and stop complaining to Dog. He doesn't understand a word, despite what you tell yourself."

It took me a couple of run-throughs to understand why

we were going to Norfolk to see Efa's brother-in-law's family. They're clearly important to her. And to Eira. And if it's important to Efa, it's important to me. She spoke about Norfolk so fondly, I thought it might be the perfect place to propose.

A car approaching catches our attention, and we all turn to see Eira and Dax pulling up. Over the last few weeks, we've seen them a lot. First, they came to New York, and then Efa seemed to be on one long, constant video call with her sister. In the last week, we've been spending time with them in London. We're in a hotel—for market research, and because Efa and I make a lot of noise when we fuck. I'm not sorry about it.

Efa and Eira hug each other like we all didn't have dinner together last night.

"Hear you're going to propose on this trip," Dax says as he shakes my hand.

I smooth my hand up my jaw. "Oh good, it will be a surprise for everyone."

Dax chuckles. "Welcome to the family."

"Speaking of, will all your brothers be here?"

He nods. "And my cousin Vincent. Since Eira and I got together, they've all made an extra-special effort to be here for occasions that matter to her, Efa, and Dylan. The three of them were on their own for a long time. But not anymore. They're Coves now." He pats me on the shoulder. "You too. It's like being part of the mafia. There's no escape."

Carole interrupts us. "Are you talking about when you're going to propose? Do you want to do it in front of everyone? That's what Dax did."

Yup, everyone knows my plan. Efa warned me that she couldn't live with secrets and she's always true to her word.

"No offense, Carole, but I've only just met you and—"

"Tish tish! We'll be family by the time John pours the second glass of malbec. But propose how you wish, just don't leave it until Sunday. We want time to celebrate with you both."

"You like malbec?" I ask. "I know this great little vineyard in Argentina. Finca Colo. If I'd known, I'd have brought some."

Dax laughs and so does Carole. "Vincent owns that vineyard. We have plenty of the stuff."

"Yeah, don't ever buy it. You're just making a rich man ever richer," Dax says.

I get the feeling no one in this family is going to care who my mother was, or that I'm rich and successful. They just care I make Efa happy. I take a deep breath. I think I'm going to enjoy it here in Norfolk with the best skies.

"You okay?" Efa asks as she comes up beside me.

"I hear I'm proposing to you this weekend."

She grins at me. "Well, aren't you?"

"You don't think it would be nice to have a surprise?"

"Bennett, I've known you were going to propose to me from the minute I saw you on the cover of *Forbes*. It's not a secret. We don't have those, remember?"

This is why Efa needed me to announce to the world that I was Ben Fort. Because she can't help but be exactly who she is. She's authentic to her core. It's only one of the reasons I love her.

"Do you want to see the ring in advance?" I ask her.

"Don't be silly," she says. "I know whatever you've picked will be incredible."

I'm a little concerned that it will be a little *too* incredible. Efa's not a showy person, yet there's no doubt the ring I've picked is... noticeable. I just want to give her the best of everything. The ring is a symbol of my desire to make our life together as special as I can.

"I hope you like it."

"I love it already," she reassures me.

"So let's have dinner tonight, then go sit under the stars and I'll ask you officially to be my wife."

"I like that plan," she says. "I like every plan that means you and I are together."

I have no doubt how Efa feels for me. But if I ever wanted confirmation, I can just listen to the way she talks about her love for me or her need to be near me. She's unabashed. And she's home to me now. And whether we end up in New York or Norfolk, as long as I'm with her, life will be perfect.

Every day I fall a little more in love with her. No doubt I'll keep falling for the rest of my life.

A Month Later

Efa is pacing in front of me and it's setting me on edge. We're still at the Mandarin Oriental—Efa refused to go back to The Avenue and have Marcella service the suite for her. Instead we tip a full day's wages to a woman we don't know. It doesn't make any sense, but as long as Efa's happy.

"There are too many decisions to make," she says. "Brownstone or apartment. Which dress to wear. And who of your five best friends will be your best man? And then there's the flowers, the cake—I'm overwhelmed right now."

"I'm not having a best man," I say, a little confused. "Why are you worrying about all these things?"

"Because we have so many decisions to make."

"We really don't. I don't care where we live—"

"Exactly! You're leaving it all up to me."

I get it now. I thought me telling her I'll go along with whatever she wanted was for the best. But that's not what she wants. That wasn't partnering her, it was leaving her with all the decisions.

"I think we should live in an apartment, because it's easier to leave when we go to London."

"Okay," she says. "I just don't want to feel... cramped."

"There's one overlooking the park on the Upper East Side that's ten thousand square feet. You're not going to feel cramped."

"You're right," she says. "But don't you think kids need a garden?" She's overthinking this. But that's alright. I've got her.

"We're not having kids anytime soon," I say. "We'll cross that bridge when we come to it. We can move, or the park will be across the street."

"Okay," she says on an exhale. As she moves, her hair shimmers and I wonder if she's actually mine. "Apartment overlooking the park. Good."

"And I like all three of the dresses you showed me online. Take them all."

She swipes me on the arm. "It's just wasteful. I think the gowny one is a little over the top for a registry office," she says.

"You'd make jeans and a t-shirt look over the top because you're so goddamn beautiful. But if it makes you happy, take the other two. And if it makes you feel better, you can donate them after you've worn them."

She fixes me with a look and I'm not quite sure if she wants to kill me or kiss me. "Okay," she says finally. "I like that idea."

"And I'm not having a best man."

"What?" Leo says as he arrives for our Monday night gathering.

Efa's eyes widen as if to say, *Told you so.*

"Unless I'm going to stand up there with all five of you, I'm not having a best man," I say. "There's no way I'm picking one of you over the others."

Leo picks up a beer from the bar and heads over. "I guess. Plus, aren't you only having a handful of guests? We'll all be standing at the front." He chuckles.

"Exactly."

"What about witnesses?" Efa asks. We're getting married in London and they have some weird rules.

"Oh yeah. I assumed we'd have Eira and Dylan," I say, clinking my glass against Leo's bottle. I turn back to Efa, and she's staring right at me like she's dumbstruck. "What?" I ask.

"I want you to fuck me right now. Right here."

Leo clears his throat from next to me. "This is awkward but... I'm strict about threesomes. I have to be the only dude."

Efa ignores him. "I mean it, Bennett. That's so nice of you."

"She gives you a real good incentive to keep doing nice things," Leo says. "I have to make a note of that."

"Like you need more sex," Efa says dismissively. "Give your poor penis a break now and then." Her expression is dour and mournful. "It might fall off."

Leo laughs. "You fit right in around here."

"Yes, I do," Efa says. "But Monday nights are boring as fuck. I'm going for a massage in twenty minutes."

Leo laughs. "You've done well."

"Don't I know it," I say, and we clink our beer bottles again.

"Oh, one more thing," Efa says.

"Hit me with it," I reply.

"Can we not do the wedding gift thing? What the hell am I supposed to buy for a freaking billionaire? You can buy anything you want. I was thinking we could make something for each other."

I take a breath because crafting isn't exactly my thing.

In the silence, Leo erupts with laughter. "Fuck me, can I get photographs of Bennett with a glue gun?"

Efa rolls her eyes. "Okay, maybe not make something. But I'd rather go small and sentimental than over the top. It feels unnecessary."

It doesn't feel unnecessary to me. I want to spoil Efa all the time. But if she doesn't want an expensive wedding gift, I have a key in my pocket that's burning a hole in the fabric.

"That's fine," I say. Because whatever she wants is fine. "So while we're hanging out, I should give you this?" I pull out the key from my pocket. "It's definitely not a wedding gift."

Efa eyes the key and then fixes me with a glare. "What did you do?"

I toss her the key and she catches it, then comes to sit next to me on the sofa.

"What is it?"

I angle the key ring so she can get a better look. It reads "Holford Road."

Her brows pull together. "This is a key for Eira and Dax's house?"

I shake my head, and she pulls in a breath.

"What did you do?" she repeats.

"It needs a bit of work, but I thought we'd need a base when we're in London. And Holford Road seems the place to be. I bought the house next to Eira and Dax's."

Her jaw goes slack and her eyes soften.

Thank fuck she's not mad.

"I love you, Bennett Fordham. You are really the most thoughtful man. Kind. Generous. Fucking sexy. How did I get so lucky?"

My chest inflates at her words. I never get tired of hearing how she loves me.

She crawls onto my lap and presses tiny kisses across my jawline. "Thank you."

"There's nothing I wouldn't do for you," I say. It's true. I'd spend it all on her. Give up everything. Go anywhere.

Leo clears his throat. "Seriously, guys, do you want me to disappear for ten minutes?"

Efa laughs and slides off my lap, settling onto the couch next to me. "Leo, Leo, Leo. You're doing it wrong if you think ten minutes is all we need. We'd need an hour or two. You need to find yourself a woman who you want to spend longer than ten minutes with."

Leo covers his ears. "No, no, no. Not interested in hearing how I need to fall in love from the smug couple on the sofa. I have zero interest in finding myself anyone to spend more than one night with."

"We'll see," Efa says. "I wasn't looking for Bennett." She slides her hand into mine and squeezes.

Before Leo and Efa can get into a real disagreement about Leo's approach to dating or sex or women—which happens on a semi-regular basis—Worth appears. He's followed by Fisher and Jack. They all hug Efa like she's their sister, and then it's business as usual. The TV's on, but no one is paying it much attention.

"So apparently none of us are your best man, you're making us fly three thousand miles across an ocean to watch you get married... Got any other news for us?" Leo asks.

"You're not having a best man?" Worth asks.

"Nope. It's stupid in my situation. It's a small wedding and only the best men are invited."

"Does anyone own a hotel in London?" Leo asks. "You must, Worth."

"Nope. Mine's in Boston." He shakes his head, like he can't believe his friends can't remember where his hotel is.

"Shit, so not only are we flying three thousand miles, we have to stump up for a hotel when we get there."

"Actually, no, you don't," Efa says. "My sister has paid for you all to stay at the place they're going to be married next summer."

"Did she?" I ask her. "You didn't tell me that."

Efa shrugs. "We're all family now."

It's been a long time since I had a family other than my five best friends. It feels good to have someone in my life who's going to be by my side forever. And although I don't know her extended family well, it feels like a good fit—like in another lifetime, I might have been friends with Dax and Jacob and the rest of the brothers-in-law, along with Eira and Dylan.

Life's so different than it was at the beginning of the summer. I'm a lucky bastard. Being with Efa has changed my life in ways I couldn't have even fathomed before she came along. I'm no longer in hiding, and being in the open isn't scary even if I come across a couple of paparazzi every now and then. In Efa, I've found love and friendship and laughter and, most importantly, freedom.

I'll spend the rest of my life trying to make her feel as good as I do when we're together.

LEO'S STORY is next in **The Play + The Pact = I Do**

BOOKS BY LOUISE BAY

All books are stand alone

The Boss + The Maid = Chemistry

The Player + The Pact = I Do

The Doctors Series

Dr. Off Limits

Dr. Perfect

Dr. CEO

Dr. Fake Fiancé

Dr. Single Dad

The Mister Series

Mr. Mayfair

Mr. Knightsbridge

Mr. Smithfield

Mr. Park Lane

Mr. Bloomsbury

Mr. Notting Hill

The Christmas Collection

14 Days of Christmas

The Player Series

International Player

Private Player

Dr. Off Limits

Standalones

Hollywood Scandal

Love Unexpected

Hopeful

The Empire State Series

The Gentleman Series

The Ruthless Gentleman

The Wrong Gentleman

The Royals Series

King of Wall Street

Park Avenue Prince

Duke of Manhattan

The British Knight

The Earl of London

The Nights Series

Indigo Nights

Promised Nights

Parisian Nights

Faithful

What kind of books do you like?

Friends to lovers

Mr. Mayfair

Promised Nights

International Player

Fake relationship (marriage of convenience)

Duke of Manhattan

Mr. Mayfair

Mr. Notting Hill

Dr. Fake Fiance

The Player + The Pact = I Do

Enemies to Lovers

King of Wall Street

The British Knight

The Earl of London

Hollywood Scandal

Parisian Nights

14 Days of Christmas

Mr. Bloomsbury

The Boss + The Maid = Chemistry

Office Romance/ Workplace romance

Mr. Knightsbridge

King of Wall Street

The British Knight

The Ruthless Gentleman

Mr. Bloomsbury

Dr. Perfect

Dr. Off Limits

Dr. CEO

The Boss + The Maid = Chemistry

The Player + The Pact = I Do

Second Chance

International Player

Hopeful

Best Friend's Brother

Promised Nights

Vacation/Holiday Romance

The Empire State Series

Indigo Nights

The Ruthless Gentleman

The Wrong Gentleman

Love Unexpected

14 Days of Christmas

Holiday/Christmas Romance

14 Days of Christmas

British Hero

Promised Nights (British heroine)

Indigo Nights (American heroine)

Hopeful (British heroine)

Duke of Manhattan (American heroine)

The British Knight (American heroine)

The Earl of London (British heroine)

The Wrong Gentleman (American heroine)

The Ruthless Gentleman (American heroine)

International Player (British heroine)

Mr. Mayfair (British heroine)

Mr. Knightsbridge (American heroine)

Mr. Smithfield (American heroine)

Private Player (British heroine)

Mr. Bloomsbury (American heroine)

14 Days of Christmas (British heroine)

Mr. Notting Hill (British heroine)

Dr. Off Limits (British heroine)

Dr. Perfect (British heroine)

Dr. Fake Fiancé (American heroine)

Dr. Single Dad (British heroine)

The Player + The Pact = I Do (American heroine)

Single Dad

King of Wall Street

Mr. Smithfield

Dr. Single Dad

Sign up to the Louise Bay mailing list www.louisebay/newsletter

Read more at www.louisebay.com

Printed in the USA
CPSIA information can be obtained
at www.ICGtesting.com
CBHW021828300724
12432CB00010B/91

9 781804 560334